S0-AFD-703

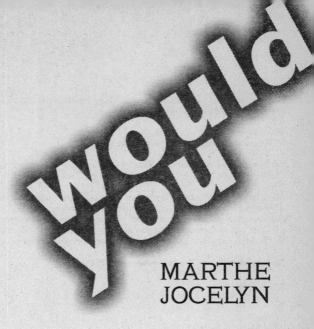

would you

MARTHE JOCELYN

Tundra Books

First mass market edition published in Canada by Tundra Books, 2010
Copyright © 2008 by Marthe Jocelyn

Published in Canada by Tundra Books,
75 Sherbourne Street, Toronto, Ontario M5A 2P9

Published in the United States by Wendy Lamb Books, an imprint of Random House
Children's Books, a division of Random House, Inc., New York

Library and Archives Canada Cataloguing in Publication

Jocelyn, Marthe
       Would you / Marthe Jocelyn.

For ages 9-12.
ISBN 978-1-77049-223-3

       I. Title.

PS8569.O254W69 2010   jC813'.54   C2009-905904-5

We acknowledge the financial support of the Government of Canada
through the Book Publishing Industry Development Program (BPIDP)
and that of the Government of Ontario through the Ontario Media Development
Corporation's Ontario Book Initiative. We further acknowledge the support
of the Canada Council for the Arts and the Ontario Arts Council for our
publishing program.

ONTARIO ARTS COUNCIL
CONSEIL DES ARTS DE L'ONTARIO

Design by Kate Gartner

Typeset in 12-point Garamond

Printed in the United States of America

1 2 3 4 5 6   15 14 13 12 11 10

For Paula
and
For all my Water Street kids

friday

A Question

Would you rather know what's going to happen? Or not know?

Getting Ready

"When did you become so *sunny*?" I ask. "You're in this perpetual good mood. Have you seen my other green flip-flop?"

Claire laughs. "I feel like . . . I feel like there's *promise*." She kicks my flip-flop out from under a heap of clothes on the floor. "It's summer. But that isn't even the best of it. I'm going to college in what, seven weeks?"

"Don't remind me. Abandoning me to face eleventh grade without your protection. Stranding me with Mom and Dad."

"Aw, Nat, don't worry." She comes over and slides her arm across my back. "You'll come for weekends sometimes. It'll be great."

"Great for you." When I think about Claire leaving, I want to throw up. We've been sharing a room since I was born. How can our life be reduced to occasional weekends?

"I have this roar in my head," she says. "Of . . . of anticipation. That it's all just starting. Stuff I don't even know about."

"Could you be any more corny?"

She ignores me, putting on mascara. They should use her eyelashes to advertise mascara.

"Where are you going tonight?" I ask.

"Movies. With Joe-boy and Kate and Mark."

"Did you fix things with Kate?"

"As long as I ignore her massive flirtation with Joe, and her relentless need to be more attractive than I am, she's the best and we're tight. Where are you going tonight?"

"Nowhere," I say. "There's nothing to do here. Summer just started and it's already boring. And so effing hot. I'll just meet everybody, I guess."

"Mwa," she says, kissing air as she grabs her bag.

"Mwa back."

Ding-Dong

They're already there when I get to the Ding-Dong, except Zack, who doesn't finish at the DQ till nine. Audrey looks pissed off, but she's still on duty. It bites to wait on your friends.

"French fries," I tell her. "Gravy on the side."

Leila is scrunched in the corner of the booth with her feet up on the seat, no matter how many times Audrey tells her, Get your stinking feet off the seat, I'll get fired if my friends mess up in here.

I slide in next to Carson. He's building a log cabin out of toothpicks. "Hey."

"Hey," they say.

Leila is filing her thumbnail with her teeth. Audrey sets down the fries, gravy poured over.

"Does the phrase *on the side* mean anything to you?"

"He wasn't listening. Just eat them, okay? Really."

"I hate using a fork for French fries," I remind her. "I like dipping."

"Get over it," says Audrey.

"They're good tonight." Carson pinches a fry. "They don't taste like cigarette butts."

"Would you rather have French fries swimming in gravy or no gravy again for the rest of your life?" says Leila, picking up her fork.

"Lame," says Carson.

"You do better." Leila flicks a crumb at his toothpick masterpiece.

"Mmmm, the point is to have options that are not options. The point is to repulse."

"Not necessarily," I say. "Moral challenge is good."

"Gravy counts as moral challenge?"

Some Good Ones from Before

Would you rather eat a rat with the fur still on or eat sewage straight from the pipe?

Would you rather have your father sing at the supermarket or your mother fart in the principal's office?

Would you rather be a murderer who gets away with it and has to live with the guilt or someone who is kidnapped by a wacko and doesn't have the courage to kill the kidnapper?

Would you rather lose all your hair or all your teeth?

Would you rather have a piece of rice permanently attached to your lip or a fly always buzzing around your head?

Would you rather be so fat you need a wheelchair to get around or so skinny your bones snap if someone bumps into you?

Would you rather die or have everyone else die?

Zack Gets Here

"I've got one," says Zack, showing up to save the day.

"Let's hear it," says Leila.

"Hello, Guh-nat," he says to me special, touching my shoulder, setting off sparks. Gnat. Nat. Get it?

"Would you rather," he says, pushing Leila's feet off the seat, "use that fork to eat a live baby or drink a pail of Mr. Harrison's acid-green pee after he's scarfed a bushel of asparagus?"

Now we're screaming. Leila's hand is over her mouth and Carson sweeps the toothpicks off the table, he's laughing so hard. Audrey races over. "Shut up, shut up, you guys!"

Mr. Harrison is the chemistry teacher, worst dandruff ever recorded in Western Hemisphere. City snowfall calculations get skewed when he shakes his head.

"Baby," we say.

"Hands down," I add. "We'll eat the baby. Pass the salt!"

"That does it," says a voice in the next booth. This woman stands up with her mouth puckered in disgust, not knowing there's a gob of ketchup on her chin. "Your behavior is appalling."

Zack stands up and bows an apology, all the cuter because he's such a nerd. He's still wearing the white paper hat he has to put on to serve ice cream. I don't mean *cute*

cute, just cute. He's skinny and freckly and he's my best friend. Except that Audrey is my best friend, but Zack's her brother. Other than when it's awkward, it's excellent to have them both in the same house.

His hair is below his collar, so they make him wear a hairnet too, but he tears that off the instant he leaves work. He likes the paper hat, though; thinks it makes a fine accessory with the patched black jeans and the skull on his T-shirt.

"Ahh," says Zack, sitting back down. "I'm done. Employment for this particular Tuesday night in history is now successfully completed. I've dug holes and I've built cones and now it's time to rest."

"How many tonight?" asks Carson.

"One hundred and twenty-three soft vanilla, eighty-nine chocolate, sixty-eight with sprinkles and a mere twenty-four with coco-crunchies."

"Thanks for the update," I say.

"If you guys are staying till I'm finished"—Audrey clicks her pen at us—"you have to order something else."

We look over to see her boss glaring from the grill, apron stiff with smears.

"Bring it on," says Zack.

Audrey nods. We all know what he's going to have after a shift at the Dairy Queen.

I get a text message from Claire: *Remind me 2 tell u what Kate said.*

Audrey brings Zack his large V8 juice with pickles on the side and a plate of saltines. Then she goes to change out of her Ding-Dong Diner Deluxe Dork uniform. We've done a survey. Of all the dumb uniforms any of us has to wear for our summer jobs, Audrey's is the worst. I secretly love my LIFEGUARD tank, but Audrey, ohmygod. She won't go outside the restaurant even to get on her bike and go straight home.

It's this pleated miniskirt with a red and white striped vest over a puffed-sleeve blousy thing made of the sleaziest polyester. Plus a little hat that has an oversized crown embroidered with the face of a clock. Audrey tells the owner that *ding-dong* means a *doorbell,* not a *clock.* She tells him, Lose the hats or rename the diner Tick-Tock. The owner's name is Bill. We call him Belly. He hates us and he doesn't listen to Audrey.

Her uniform is especially funny because she cares more about her clothes than any of us. She's all about thrift stores and sewing stuff together to make things no one else would ever think of.

Zack gets his salty fix and Audrey comes out of the bathroom. You wouldn't know it was the same girl who just went in. Milkmaid braids have been turned into a rat's nest, yellow puffed sleeves traded for shredded black silk, cheerleader skirt replaced by a piece of tapestry or something, stitched at some clever angle to sit on her hips and still hang right.

"Found a new pool today," says Zack, adding lemon and horseradish to his V8. "Everyone on bikes?"

We all nod. Sometimes we walk, but basically, how could we live without bikes? None of us can drive yet. Leila's got her beginner's, but she's not allowed to have a car full of teenaged passengers. Eventually she'll have her own car because her parents give her everything. That's her summer job, getting stuff from her parents. Sometimes that's why we like her.

"We should go," says Zack. "It's out past that minimall where the Seven-Eleven is. There's a crescent development out there where we're putting in a rockery."

"A *rockery*, Zack?" says Carson. "What the hell is a *rockery*? What the hell is a *crescent development*? Why do you know these things?"

Zack knows everything. He reads ingredients on boxes. He scans dictionaries for fun. He memorizes encyclopedias. Excuse me, encyclopediae. His phony word.

His eagerness to earn money and improve himself serves us well. He works evenings at the DQ, so we get half-price Blizzards, and he gets up at dawn to dig holes and handle the wheelbarrow for Crombie Landscape, so he knows where the pools are, essential inside information for our favorite summer pastime.

Pool-Hopping

It's summer, so we're all wearing swimsuits under our clothes. Except Leila, whose tits are too big not to wear a bra at all times. But she wears a bikini top over her bra.

Like all other sports, pool-hopping is an art. If you mess up, you can really mess up. So pay attention.

We cycle for way longer than we feel like but Zack swears it'll be worth it. Of course he gets us lost and we circle around these dumb streets like Meadowlark Crescent and Bobolink Lane, as if it's an aviary instead of a suburb. The houses will be nice in about a hundred years when the trees loom over the roofs, but now they're just new.

"Got it," says Zack. "That's the one."

"You sure?"

"Yeah, see the dirt at the sides of the drive? That's me. That's what I did today."

The drive is made of these giant cobblestones, as if some ancient Roman lives here.

"Go past, go past," hisses Audrey. She bikes ahead a couple of houses.

We park our bikes in a phalanx—keeping with the ancient-worlds motif—and do not lock. Never lock when pool-hopping. Amazingly, we haven't lost a bike yet, in a town where bicycle theft is the number-one crime.

I put my flip-flops right under the kickstand and slide out of my tee. I leave it with my shorts in the basket.

"Ready?" Audrey always acts like she's the captain, and mostly we let her.

"Ready," we all say.

"Is the gate locked, Zack? Do you think?"

"I doubt it," says Zack. "But there are bags of peat moss stacked against the fence if we need to climb over."

"Okay," says Audrey. "Go!"

We go, racing like fools, bare feet not summer-ready yet, *ouch*ing on tarmac sprinkled with construction grit.

"Ow! Ow! Ow!"

"Sssh!"

We're squeaking and giggling, panting up to the gate.

The latch is on the inside, but it's easy to open. It nearly always is. I've only had to fence-hop twice. We stream through in a swarm, buzzing with mischief.

Carson prides himself on being first, but Audrey's pretty competitive. I wait till there's space, not wanting to jump in on top of other bodies.

Splash! Splash! Splash! Spl-splash! Like stones hurled from the same fist.

In, dunk, stroke, side.

A light goes on upstairs in the house.

"Light," shouts Audrey, but we all saw it.

I boost myself out, dripping, and the others are already running. Leila's limping, must have banged a knee or something. We're making enough racket to wake a drunk.

I'm last through the gate. A light comes on downstairs and we peel toward the bikes, laughing instead of breathing.

The front door opens. "Hey!"

I jam on my flip-flops, grab my tee, throw a leg over, push off and kick away the kickstand in one motion. I am unstoppable. My butt is soaking wet and slippery on the seat.

"Hey! You there! Hey! Damn kids!"

We zoom away from the house, back into the maze of Birdland, with the hollow shouts behind us and the glee of trespass making us bark like a pack of dogs in the curving, sleeping streets.

Later

Downtown, only Beanie's Coffee Bar is open, and the Donut Barn. We see Claire outside the cinema saying goodbye to Kate.

"Claire," I call. "Claire."

"Hey." She comes riding over.

"Where's Joe?" I ask. "What did you see?"

"Joe left," she says. "We saw the one the boys wanted. Really dumb. But it had a good chase scene and a happy ending."

"Oh," says Zack. "You mean girls like the ones that slow down and end in tears?"

Claire laughs. "Where you going?"

"Swimming," we say. "Wanna come?"

"Swimming? You mean . . . ?"

"Yeah."

"Where?"

"You want to come with us?" I say. She never has. Usually, my friends are too young, not cool enough.

"Yay, Claire," says Zack. "Come."

I get this clutching in my chest. I'm pretty sure Claire and Zack had sort of a thing. Not a real whole thing, but maybe a time or two a while ago when they hooked up. I used to ask myself, Would you rather not see him ever again or see him every day with your sister? Zack is a year older than me and a year younger than her. They were on the same team from our school for the Smart Teen Challenge, and I know he really liked her. Then she got with Joe-boy and maybe Zack felt like the loser.

But now he's saying, "Come with us, Claire," and she's giving him that warm, sweet smile.

"Why not?" she says. "I might as well try it once in my life, right?"

And we all say, *"Right!",* like we've converted another sucker to our cult.

A minute later she clubs the brake. "I'm not wearing a swimsuit."

"That's okay," we all say.

"Undies work," says Audrey. "We're only going to Amanda Layton's, clothing optional."

"The perfect starter operation," says Zack.

Amanda Layton is a folksinger who has a pool and a hot tub. She's nearly always away on tour, playing music festivals and hippie conventions. We can't figure out who buys her CDs, but somebody must because she's got this vast house. The pool is no challenge, really, except for one nosy neighbor who clearly wants to come in herself.

Claire does fine. We linger in the water, floating, stargazing, no worries until the neighbor's patio door slides open and we hightail it out of there. We're all cheering Claire, high on fun for a few minutes. Then she brakes.

"I left my wallet," she says. "I took it out of my pocket. It's on the bench by the hot tub."

"I'll go back with you," says Zack.

"No, I'll just go," says Claire. "I'll catch up with you later."

The Cops

So we're zipping down King Street in a pack and we see the cruiser behind us.

"Dang," says Audrey, Western drawl. "Looks like the sheriff done nosed us out."

We slow down but keep going, not really thinking there's trouble. We're not doing anything wrong. At the moment. But then the siren goes *blip, blip*, telling us to stop. We stop.

Two officers climb out. One is Burt McCafferty, who coaches Claire's soccer team, and the other one I don't know.

"Hello, kids," says Burt.

"Hello." We're all bright and peppy the way cops want kids to be, not mumbly and shifty-eyed and high on illegal substances.

"This here is Officer Foster," says Burt. "Just moved to town from Oakdale."

"Hello, Officer Foster," we singsong, like he's visiting our second-grade class to tell us about traffic rules.

"Where you coming from?" says Burt. "Why are you all wet?"

"We were swimming," says Leila. "At my house."

"Oh really?"

"Yeah."

"Your parents home?"

We look at Leila, since none of us knows. Even though if we'd just been there we would know. If they were out, we'd still be there, eating all the ice cream sandwiches in the freezer. If they'd been home, we would have noticed. We would have said, Hey, Mrs. Greyson, how are you? The garden looks nice this year.

"They might be home by now," says Leila, trying to cover both angles.

"We had a call," says Burt. "Didn't we, Foster?"

"Yep," says the other guy, growly-like. "Citizens complaining about a break-in."

Citizens? What TV show do these guys think they're starring in? We straddle our bikes, not looking at each other.

"Break-in?" I say, because it's too quiet.

"Over in the new development," says Burt. "Break and entry in the backyard pool."

"Oh," says Leila. "That's a break and entry? I thought you had to break something, like a window. Or a vase."

Audrey snorts. "A vase, Leila?"

"This is not a laughing matter, young lady," says Officer Foster.

"We don't want to think it's anything to do with you folks," says Burt. "You're good kids, I know you kids. But you're all wet."

"We were swimming," says Leila. "At my house."

"And where *is* your house?" asks Officer Foster.

"Burt's been there," says Leila, showing off. "For dinner. It's on Caledonia Street."

"So where are you headed now?" he says.

"Donut Barn," says Carson.

"The Beanie," says Audrey.

"We're just biking everyone home," I say, "But we're stopping for snacks along the way."

Claire picks that moment to come steaming along.

"Hey," she says, grinning all round. "Hi, Coach Cop."

I make bug eyes at her so she pays attention.

"Did you find your wallet that you went back to Leila's for?" I ask.

She tilts her head at me. I tilt back. She puts her hand in her shorts pocket and pulls out a soggy wallet.

"It fell in a puddle," she says, smooth as a new-shaved leg.

"Beside the pool?" says Burt.

"Lotta splashing going on," says Claire.

"You were with these kids tonight, Claire?" asks Burt. Like she's a chaperone.

"Yes, sir," she says. "Trying to squeeze some sister time into the last few weeks before I go away."

"Good for you," says Burt, patting her shoulder. He turns to us, all paternal.

"Don't let us see you kids again tonight," he says. Officer Foster grunts, like he's not fooled. But he doesn't know Claire, doesn't know that with Burt McCafferty, Claire's word is like a pledge carved on a shield.

I'm surprised she lied so easily. Normally she's kind of upstanding. Teacher's pet material.

"I forgot to tell you," she says on the way home. "What Kate said."

"What?"

"She said she thought you were going to be prettier than me. Someday."

"Typical Kate," I say. "Insult us both with the same compliment."

Claire laughs. "No, I think she actually meant it the good way."

"Don't worry," I say. "She's wrong."

saturday

The Y

There's this moment whenever I get to work and stand beside the pool, before the surface is broken. The water is so blue and so calm it seems to actually reflect the sky, instead of just holding a thousand quarts of chlorine. Makes me want to *slip* in with hardly a ripple, to immerse myself in liquid turquoise.

But then the morning shift begins. I crank up the music till the AquaFifties Plus think they're reliving their junior years in a dance club. Marlene and Liz and Joan and Phyllis, all my regular fatties, kicking and splashing, working up to the frosty mocha cappuccino and sour cream glazed at the Donut Barn.

Then in come the children, herded by mothers in varying degrees of annoying.

I go, "Hey, Tadpoles! Hey, Otters!"

Shannon takes the Otters to the other side and I get into the pool for the first time today. Now that it's stirred up, the water looks way too used. I have to make a dunking seem fun for the Tadpoles huddled on the side. The brave ones have their legs in already, whacking at the surface to make foam. It takes most of the thirty-minute lesson to coax them all in, holding on to the side for dear life.

Tadpoles are the cutest, though. When they get as old as Seals and Dolphins, those kids are brats. But even with demon children drowning each other and peeing in the pool, lessons win over laps anytime.

Watching laps bites.

There's this old man about eighty years old, or more, maybe. He's had the swim trunks for half his life, I swear. They're the color of dry dirt and tied on with string. I don't even want to think about what if the string breaks. He's got yellowy nails that curl over the end of his toes like he's some prehistoric reptile.

He comes at 11:59 for the noon lap swim and takes ten minutes to get down the ladder. Then it takes him fifteen to paddle his way from this end of the pool to the other. We call him Driftwood. We take bets on his time. He's so slow it's mesmerizing. I've been tricked more than once into thinking he's dead in the water. He stops moving and floats along, as if there's a current. And I'm going, Please no, I have to do mouth-to-mouth on Driftwood?

After Work

I go to Audrey's after my job, before her job. We have an hour to lie in her backyard as naked as we can get, wearing screw-you-ozone oil, SPF 4. Zack's not here because he's digging in somebody's garden or serving ice cream. So it's just us, hanging.

"If I had my eyebrows shaved off completely," I say, "I'd have such a great tan line."

"Mmmm," says Audrey. "Let's consider that for our initiation ceremony."

"Initiation to what?"

"To our club."

"What club?"

"Let's start a club."

Who's Hot, Who's Not

The guy next door turns on his lawn mower and Audrey groans.

"Mr. Buckle is pornographically fixated on his lawn," she says. "I'm not kidding, every Saturday, he gets practically horizontal to pick up twigs."

"And you call him Buckle because?"

"His belt buckle is always open, swear to God. I'll give you five dollars if you look over that fence right now and his buckle is done up."

"I'm not risking it," I say. "But isn't he the guy with Hot Jimmy for a son? The boy who works the bar at O'Dooleys?"

"He's not as hot as the new Pizza Shack guy," says Audrey, flipping over. "And definitely not hot enough to overcome the idea of ever having a conversation with his father."

"Are parents really relevant?" I ask.

"Parents are *so* relevant," says Audrey. "How else are you going to know if the guy will be bald someday?"

"Bald is so wrong," I agree.

"And don't you think parents should be considered when selecting a life mate?" says Audrey. "What about Thanksgiving?"

"Whoa! That question is loaded with flaws."

"As in?"

"You don't select a mate the way you choose a shampoo, Audrey. They're not all lined up in front of you at the same time displaying themselves for possible selection. And why are you using the phrase *life mate*? There shouldn't even be such a thing."

"Too true," says Audrey. "Who wants to be stuck with the same guy?"

"For *life*," I say. "For*ever*. All you have to do is look at any of our parents to know what a pointless concept it is."

"My point exactly," says Audrey.

"What? That parents are relevant?"

"Yes."

"As the lowest rung of comparison, maybe."

What If

"What if," says Audrey. "What if I got turned into an insect but you could hear me speak and I was still the same person, but I was an insect."

"What kind of insect?"

"Something benign."

"A praying mantis?"

"Sure." Audrey rolls over and lunges for the sunblock.

"Well, I'd keep you in my room . . . on my dresser, maybe, so you could see in the mirror. And I'd talk to you. But it really wouldn't be the same."

"No kidding."

Worst Words

"What's your all-time worst word?" Audrey starts a new game.

"No discussion. The worst word is *moist. Moist!* Could anything be more explicit? *Mmmmooyysssst.*"

"Ew!" says Audrey. "And I hate *mustache,* don't you? Isn't that just nasty? I hate the thing and I hate the word."

"How about a moist mustache?" I say. "The bald gynecologist had a moist mustache."

"*Ew!*"

"Oh, and another one," I say. "*Dangling*. What about *dang-guh-ling?*"

"Ew! Ew! Extreme ew!"

Audrey has to get ready for work. Her uniform, naturally, is at the Ding-Dong, but she combs her hair.

Getting Ready Again

Probably should make it an early night except that Mom says I should be in early, meaning I'm staying out late. But nobody has any ideas for what to do anyway, so tonight is going to bite.

Claire's in front of the only full-length mirror, and I'm waiting, barely. She's not even dressed and she's *loitering;* just to make me insane.

"Have you seen my black thingy?" she says.

"What black thingy?"

"You know, my *black* thingy."

She leaves the mirror to look again in the closet, in the drawers, on the floor, under the bed.

I examine myself while I watch her in the glass.

"With straps," she says, "The one I got at Sheba's Thrift. I've been planning to wear it all week."

"Meh." I'm noncommittal. "Where are you going, anyway?"

"Party at Terry's. You?"

"Nowhere. Ding-Dong to start."

"Did you take my black thing? Did you wear it to Audrey's and leave it there? 'Cause if you did, I'll kill you."

"No, I did not wear it and leave it at Audrey's," I say.

" 'Cause she'll cut off the bottom or change the straps or something, and it's the one thing that I–"

"Claire, shut up. It's not at Audrey's."

"Well, where is it, Nat?"

I go into the bathroom, shrugging. I wish I had a party to go to.

The light is better in here for makeup. My hair is good tonight; skin too, for a change. What a waste.

Claire comes in and gives me a hip check so she has room over the sink. She's wearing a white V-neck shirt and her haircut from before the prom still looks so good.

"You look nice," I say, not saying she looks too gorgeous for words. I squelch my vile, bitter envy. Her life is going to explode. She's going away!

"Joe-boy better be worried about the swarm of boys waiting for you at school," I say.

Her eyes meet mine in the mirror. "I'm breaking up with him tonight."

"What? But he adores you!"

"Mmmm," she says. "If by *adore* you mean *behave like a bloodsucking leech around.*"

"Does Kate know?"

"This has nothing to do with Kate. He's been kind of

bugging me. He's all morbid about me leaving. He's acting clingy and annoying and . . . and *young*. I want to have my summer without all the stress of saying goodbye. And then I want to just leave, you know?"

"Wow," I say. "He's not going to like this."

"I'll be gentle," she laughs.

"What's the point of no curfew," I say, "if there's nowhere to go? This town is *so boring*!"

Claire grins at me and uses Dad's voice. "An intelligent person is *never* bored."

I punch her shoulder and she punches me back.

"Ow!"

"Gotta go," she says. "Joe's waiting."

"For the last time," I say.

"Mwa!" She goes.

"Bye."

Poor Joe, I'm thinking.

I pull off my gray sweater and untuck her black thingy from my jeans. It looks great. But she doesn't have to know that.

DQ

We're sitting in a row on the concrete divider between the Dairy Queen parking lot and the Cosmos Launderama parking lot. Zack just got off work, but too late to catch the late movie. Nobody really wants to go anyway. We usually wait for Twofer Tuesdays. We still have about an hour until it's dark enough to go pool-hopping.

Carson is on a roll. "What if someone told you the world was going to end? What would you do in the last three days before the end?"

"Is your source a credible one?" asks Zack. "Or counter-factual?"

"Christ, Zack! Let's say the world is going to end. What do you do with the time left?"

"I'd go skydiving," says Leila.

"I'd tell everyone what I really think of them," says Audrey.

"Oh, like you don't do that already?" Carson has been the recipient of many an Audrey earful.

"I think I'd sit really still," I say. "And watch everybody else flip out."

"Lame," says Carson.

"Okay, what would you do?"

"I'd have sex, of course. With twenty or thirty different girls, and no fear of STDs 'cause the world is going to end anyway."

"And where are you going to find twenty or thirty girls whose last wishes include having sex with Carson Jefferson?" I ask him. "Where are you going to find *one*?"

"Oh, I'd find them."

"You need a taste of reality, Carson."

"I love reality! Especially when it's on TV."

"And then let's say your source is proved wrong," says Zack. "It was all a hoax and the world is not going to end. Then what would you do?"

"Go straight to the doctor."

"I'd be glad I told people what I think of them," says Audrey. "Anyone who can't take the truth shouldn't be using up oxygen on my planet."

"Well, aren't we supposed to do that anyway?" says Leila. "Live every day as if it's our last? You know, fully?"

"Fear of public speaking and fear of getting fat are way above fear of death in opinion polls," says Zack. "Fear of deformed people and fear of making mistakes are also up there."

"And that is relevant because?" says Audrey.

"Depends on how you're going to die," I say.

This inspires Carson. "Would you rather be attacked by a huge genetically engineered plus environmental-fiasco spider *or* be up against a ruthless, brilliant assassin who was under orders to take you dead or alive?"

Audrey groans. "I *hate* movies where there's a blob for an enemy—there's no challenge, no psychology. With a human being there's always a chance you might just—"

"Oh that's so typical of a girl," says Carson. "You think you could just use sex to save your life."

"Oh that's so typical of a boy," says Audrey. "You represent the decades of sexist pigs who've created the cultural stereotype of an imprisoned woman bargaining with her charms to save her life, and then you turn around and act like there's something wrong with it. Like you wouldn't let someone out of jail for a blow job?"

"Uh, gee, Audrey, now that you mention it . . ."

We push him to the ground and throw gravel all over his perfect white T-shirt.

Police Activity

We manage to kill a couple of hours, just riding around rearranging people's porch furniture. We're coming home cheerful and we pass Devon Road. A cruiser is parked sideways across the end of the street. There are lights and extra cops and one of those yellow plastic ribbons being stretched around pylons.

"Good," says Audrey. "Keep the officers busy while the teenage delinquents wreak mayhem all over town."

"Havoc, Audrey. Wreak havoc."

We split up at the corner and I head for home.

The Phone Call

My cell is ringing as I turn onto our block. I pull it out of my back pocket but it's only HOME, so I don't answer. I'm nearly there anyway.

I put my bike in the garage and pull down the rusting,

rattling door. The kitchen light is on. Actually, every light in the house seems to be on. Bit late for them, isn't it?

My cell rings again. I go in the back door with it still ringing. Dad's at the wall phone and Mom is at the table with her head in her hands. One look and I feel thunder in my brain. There's something really wrong.

How the World Turns in a Heartbeat

I look at them and they look at me. Dad hangs up the phone and my cell stops ringing. He half smiles but then shrugs and his face scrunches up like someone poked him in the eye.

"What?" I say.

"It's Claire," he whispers.

"Claire," says Mom. She scrapes the chair back and stumbles up. Her eyes look wild, extra blue. She opens her arms and I walk into them.

"Claire what?"

I pull out of the hug and Mom slumps back down on the chair with her face hidden in her hands.

"There's been an accident," says Dad.

"Oh," I say, "we might have passed it. On Devon Road?"

"They didn't say where," says Dad.

"What? You mean Claire?"

"Claire has been hit by a car."

There's not enough air for a second.

"Is she . . . is she alive?"

"She's very seriously injured," says Dad. "They say. We were trying to reach you before we go to the hospital."

"We should go now." Mom jumps up. "We have to see Claire." She snatches her bag from a chair but it flies out of her hand.

Dad puts his arm around her, trying to slow things down, but she jerks away and cries, "Now! We have to go now!"

"I'm coming too," I say. They look at me, ready to say no, but how could they say no?

I am swamped with a clammy sweat. My bathing suit's still wet under my clothes.

"I have to pee," I say. "I'll meet you out front." I race to the stairs. Claire was hit by a car. No way. Claire was hit by a car. For real?

Claire's wardrobe tornado is still all over the room. I peel off my swimsuit and toss it in the tub while I pee. I put on underwear, put my damp clothes back on. I'm wearing Claire's black thing. I'll wear it to the hospital, show her I've got it, confess. The horn beeps; I fly down the stairs. Dad said "very seriously injured." What does that mean? What the *hell* does that mean?

They Make Us Wait

When we say Claire's name to the reception nurse in Emergency, she says "Oh" and looks around in a panic, like she needs someone to help her. Or maybe I'm making that up because the place is freaking me out.

"If you'll take a seat," she says. "Someone will be right with you."

"We're not taking a seat," says Dad. He's tall anyway, but he's making the nurse shrink.

"I need to see my little girl," says Mom.

"It's the family," says the nurse into a phone, like there's only one family, like everyone knows.

"Is she still alive?" I ask.

"Yes," says the nurse. "She's inside, in the trauma bay. Someone will be out to speak with you shortly."

We stand there waiting. Maybe it's not so long, but it feels like forever. At least five minutes. Like holding a baking pan without an oven mitt for at least five minutes.

There's a lady in one of the seats, clutching her wrist and whimpering. There's an old guy wearing an undershirt and wrinkled khakis. He's sitting on the coffee table instead of a chair, his hands fumbling around, not finding his knees to rest on.

New game, I think. Guess the Emergency. But I don't see anything wrong with him, so maybe there's a wrinkly wife in her nightie somewhere behind that swinging door.

I notice how I'm not breathing and then I breathe and I notice I can't hear anything except a buzz in my ears from brain cells colliding.

My mother is pacing in circles like a maniac panther. Dad is this huge silent lump leaning against the wall next to me, with his shoulder half covering a sign: HAVE INSURANCE CARDS READY BEFORE SPEAKING TO RECEPTION.

The First Doctor of Many

A doctor wearing green scrubs comes out. I recognize the scene from TV, only he's not handsome and he has a bristly neck.

"Mr. and Mrs. Johnson?"

They swish to attention, like startled puppets.

"You are Claire's next of kin? Your daughter is not married?"

"No, no, it's us," they tell him.

The doctor looks at me.

"I'm her sister."

He looks nervous, with bloodshot eyes.

"I'm Dr. David Cooper," he says. "I'm a resident here at the hospital. What I have to say will be difficult to hear. Claire has been very badly hurt. We're monitoring the situation closely. She has had a severe head injury and is not responding to stimuli at this time. She may have some bleeding in her brain."

He pauses while Mom sags against Dad. "We're work-ing at the moment to stabilize her vitals. We had to wait for Dr. Hazel—he's the neurosurgeon—to come back in, but he's here now and we're preparing her for surgery."

"Can we see her?" asks Mom.

"In a few minutes," says Dr. Cooper. He looks for refuge on the pages pinned to his clipboard. I'm guessing he hasn't done this too often, this talking-to-the-family-in-a-traumatic-crisis-hell situation.

"I need to ask you a few questions. Does Claire have any health issues we should know about? Is she diabetic, for instance? Or does she have an allergy to any medica-tions?"

"No," says Dad. "She's the healthiest girl alive."

Dr. Cooper blinks a couple of times.

Not anymore, I can hear him thinking.

"I see." He writes something down. "Did any of you witness the accident?"

We all murmur no, shaking our heads. I wonder for the first time who *did* see it. Who called?

"Is anyone else hurt?" I ask.

He doesn't look at me. "I'm not at liberty to tell you that," he says. I glance around, maybe to see Kate's par-ents, or Joe's, but then I remember the nurse saying, It's *the* family, like there's only one.

"How old is Claire?" asks Dr. Cooper.

"Eighteen," say Mom and Dad together.

The doctor's pencil hesitates. "Oh."

"What, 'Oh'?" I don't like the way he said "Oh."

Dad pats my shoulder.

"I think the doctor means that Claire is not a minor, am I right?"

"What difference does that make? Shouldn't you be in there saving her?" I say. "Aren't these questions kind of pointless?"

"There may be certain decisions," says Dr. Cooper, "about her treatment. If she were a minor, your parents would have to make them. As it is . . ."

"Can you just tell us the situation?" says Dad.

Dr. Cooper ducks his eyes. He can't look at us during the next part.

"It seems that Claire, after impact, somersaulted and landed a distance away from the collision site. She apparently had a seizure on the spot. She has a broken collarbone and several other injuries. Most importantly, she has suffered severe trauma to the head and brain."

He stops. *Severe trauma to the head and brain.*

"Can we see her?" asks Mom.

Spin Mode

We follow Dr. Cooper through the swinging doors and he sticks us in this room by ourselves, as if he's considering our privacy, but really it's just the Bad Effing News Room.

Dad pulls Mom into a hug.

"Come on," he says to me. "Let's have a Lump."

So I go over and let him fold me in too.

"Knock, knock," says a nurse, coming in. "I'm Sue. You're Claire's family? I do triage."

We all just look at her. Triage?

"We're preparing Claire for surgery, but you'll be able to see her for a minute before we take her in. She could be in there for, well, a few hours, maybe, depending on how it goes. I'm going to warn you, there are several tubes, intravenous lines and cardiac monitor wires all in place. We've put her on a ventilator. She's not in good shape and it might be alarming for you to see her, but—"

"We're coming," says Mom, and she's out the door right behind Sue, with Dad at her heels.

I'm not so sure.

I see where they're going, and I see the rolling gurney thing. And I see the shape of a body under a draped sheet. I see extra carts with machines on them, and tubes and hookups and bags hanging there. . . . All these people are moving like mechanical dolls.

I stay back while Mom and Dad go right over and Sue is saying something, but all I can really see is a hand sort of curled inside the railing of this bed on wheels.

That's Claire?

Mom picks this moment to fall to the floor in a heap. I don't know if she fainted or took one look and just couldn't stand up anymore. She's on the floor and there's a silent pause and then she starts to howl. Dad bends over, trying to soothe her, rubbing her arms. She wrenches away and wails. I'm just watching, hot all over, mostly behind the eyeballs. My mother has lost her mind. What am I supposed to do? I've never seen anything like this.

"Mom?" I creep closer. The medical people are zooming around, pushing Claire's bed out of the way through some doors and gone.

I don't know what to do. But neither does Sue or Dr. Cooper. I hear the murmurs; they're going to give Mom drugs.

I want to start screaming too but I can't breathe, can't breathe in to scream out.

I sit on the floor next to Dad. Mom is kneeling, rocking a little, holding herself.

"Mom." I'm afraid to touch her, so I just lean in close. "Mom," I whisper. She catches her next noise before it comes out. She hears me and she's trying to stop, I can see that.

"Mom," I say, really slowly, inches away. "They're going to see if they can fix her."

Mom puts out a hand and finds my face. She shudders a couple of times.

"I'm sorry," she says. We wait. "It's a shock." We wait some more. "I'm all right now." She opens her eyes and climbs upright.

Now We're Part of Some System

They put us in this other room and a woman comes in. She's shorter than I am and kind of lumpy.

"Hello," she says. "I'm Janet Fox. You're the family of Claire Johnson? I'm your social worker."

My father spins on her. "A *social* worker? What for? Don't bother us with any head-shrinking crap right now, okay?"

Instead of ducking, Janet Fox is easy and calm. "I can appreciate that this is all very scary, Mr. Johnson. My concern right now is to make sure you all have something warm to drink."

For the first time I notice that my mother is shivering. And nodding. "Yes," she says. "Do you have any coffee?"

"Right away," says Janet Fox. And then to me, "How about some hot chocolate?"

I shrug. "Okay."

Dad shakes his head. He pulls out his cell phone but stuffs it back into his pocket right away, like he can't face what using it will mean.

"If there's anyone you'd like me to call?" Janet Fox pauses in the doorway. "That's something else I'm good at."

"Oh, dear god," says my mother. She hunches over in the chair, so her face is on her knees. Janet Fox darts to a cabinet and takes out a blanket. She lays it across my mother's back.

"Keep her warm," she says to my dad. "I'll get the coffee."

Mom is shaking as if there's a chill wind, but there's no air to breathe.

"Let's go home," I say when the door closes. Dad nods at me.

"No," Mom croaks. "I'm staying here."

"Honey, they said it'll be several hours. We're a mile away," Dad tells her. "We'll come back."

"I'm staying." Mom pulls the blanket tight around her shoulders. Her hair is sticking out and the gray roots are kind of obvious. I try to smooth it down for her. She takes my hand and holds it against her cheek.

I look at Dad. "I'll take you home," he says. "But I'll make sure that woman or somebody is here with her while I'm gone."

"I'm waiting outside," I say. I run for the door, imagining that I'll burst into the parking lot and there'll be fresh air to drink in gulps. But it's hotter out here than inside, and the night hasn't moved since we arrived.

The Police

There's a cruiser with flashing lights sitting by the entrance. Officer McCafferty and that new guy look at me through the windshield and then look at each other. Coach Cop rubs a hand over his face and climbs out like I'm an ugly blind date. Dad comes through the door behind me at the same time.

"Burt," says Dad.

"Mr. Johnson," says Coach Cop.

"Oh," says Dad, figuring out that this is somehow official.

"Can we go back in?" Burt McCafferty takes Dad's arm. "I'm afraid we have to ask some questions."

How I Finally Get to Sleep

I lie across the hood of the car, waiting. The metal is half a degree cooler than the air against my cheek, soothing, like the smooth deck of a pool after a long swim.

Dad comes out and we get in the car.

He drives so slowly we could be walking. Then he brakes. His hands are trembling on the wheel.

"Are you okay?" I ask.

"I just need a minute," he says. "I'm feeling kinda shaky."

I go to hit the radio button out of habit but I stop in time. How bad taste would that be, eh?

We get home in silence.

"We forgot to lock the door," he says as we go in. "There's someone to blame for this, Natalie." And he purposely kicks over a kitchen chair in the near dark.

I pick it up and he kicks over another one.

"Jesus, Dad." I hold my breath. What next? What display of parental insanity is next?

But he just turns on the light and tosses his keys into the basket on the counter.

He's going to pick up a book and stuff, a sweater for Mom, and go back in an hour. I lie on the couch while he wanders around. I watch TV with the remote on my leg, exactly within fingertip distance, clicking every time a thought sneaks into my brain.

Click.

Some kind of documentary dog show, where we see them getting bathed and shampooed. Was it this morning I had a shift at the Y?

Click.

Law & Order.

Dad keeps bumping into chairs or tripping over the rug. He's shuffling, picking things up and putting them down. "That car wasn't driving itself," he mutters.

Click.

Another stupid model show with selfish bitchy girls dissing each other while trying on thongs. What would they do if one of their perfect bodies got crushed by a Honda Civic?

Click.

"Somersault?" says Dad suddenly.

Uh-oh.

"She didn't know how to somersault! The only kid at

Playtime Pals who couldn't *do* a somersault! That's why she played soccer instead of gymnastics!"

Click.

"This is how you're gonna spend the night?" says Dad.

"Mmmm."

"I'm going back to the hospital. Go to bed."

"Uh-huh."

I'm too tired to go to bed. Too wired. I find this channel that is selling a knife that can cut anything: tomatoes, cardboard, hard-boiled eggs, frozen dinner rolls and ham bones. I watch and watch and watch. Wow, we should get one of these.

I go upstairs around morning. I crawl into Claire's bed, which is not exactly made, and I flip the pillow over. I pull up the duvet and I curl into the smallest kitten ball I can get into. And I go to sleep.

sunday

Morning Comes at, Like, Noon

Now I know what *like zombies* really means. We sit at the breakfast table like zombies with no discernible brain function. But then I think, Oh god, what if Claire is a zombie?

We're each bent over a cup of coffee, but no one bothers to steam milk or pour juice or toast an English muffin. I move the telephone ringer to silent. We don't hear the ring but we hear the machine bleep and pick up. After about the fourth time, I turn the recording to silent too. The radio is not on, so no Mozart or any of those other guys in wigs. Usually Mom and Dad would be doing the Sunday crossword right now, speaking in code: *Seven letters starting with* C-O- . . .

But instead, we're huddled like refugees on a dock. What are we supposed to do? Act like normal people?

How It Went

Dad tells me he was drooling and Mom was asleep with her head on his lap when they came to say that all efforts had been made to salvage Claire's brain. The bleeding in her head had been evacuated, her broken bones had been set, she was being pumped full of saline, and Mrs. Johnson should go home to get some rest. Dad brought her home, but no rest yet.

"The men in the ambulance said she was conscious for a minute or two," says Mom. "After the accident. One of them said, 'If a person is talking, you can be pretty sure she's breathing.'"

Mom had an injection, Dad told me. A sedative. That's why she sounds so careful.

"Claire was talking when they got there, but no one could tell me what the words were. I wish I knew what she . . ." Her voice catches and two tears run gently down her face. She doesn't even wipe them away.

Dad puts a hand under Mom's elbow and seems to lift her up. They leave their coffee cups on the table and shamble out of the kitchen. I think he's going to put her to bed. She looks like a little old lady, leaning on him, the backs of her arms freckled and shaking.

I wait till the thumps upstairs are settled.

I write a note: *Gone to see Claire. Took my bike. N.*

First Time

The nurse has colored hair, something like Pumpkin Kool-Aid. Her name tag says TRISHA.

"I'm going to let you start with five minutes," she says, not thinking about how it may be the most intense five minutes of my life. Or maybe avoiding thinking about it. She's been here and seen this a hundred times, or a thousand. I've been here once. Maybe her whole life is looking at families whacked in the face with trauma. So maybe, to be fair, she's protecting me.

Trauma—our new state of being.

There's a ceremony first. Trisha shows me how to wash my hands, how to put on the smock and the gloves and the mask. It's like on TV, all the papery garments, only I'm trembling and the clothes shiver and crackle.

"You are not to touch her," says Trisha. "You are to stay two feet from the bed at all times. She's very vulnerable to infection. You are not to cough or sneeze. You are not to touch any of the tubes or the equipment. You are most especially not to touch her."

"What *can* I do?" I say.

"Some people talk," she says, not so bossy now. "Some people just sit. There's research showing that if you talk she may hear you. It may be of some comfort to tell her things. Say her name a lot. Remind her who she is. It might even trigger a repair mechanism. It's a long, slow process, so don't be disappointed if there's no response." She taps her watch. "Five minutes."

The Five Minutes

The overhead lights, the fluorescent ones, are off. It's dim in here and you're on the bed.

Claire. It's you but not you. Your hair is all gone. They shaved your head and there's this, this, oh god, it's awful, a huge *injury* on the side of your skull, swollen, with black crisscrossed stitches, holding together this *gash*, not bandaged or anything, just there for us to look at. Horrible.

Your eyes are closed. Good. I was afraid of looking into vacant eyes. You definitely don't want to see this.

The nurse said maybe, if anything's ticking, maybe you can hear me. Maybe you're just . . . gathering strength.

Wow. Claire.

It's hard to . . . believe.

This is the way you look now. Yesterday we were getting ready to go out and . . . I mean, *yesterday*, you know? And I stole your black thing . . . and then you . . . didn't come home.

Claire? Please, Claire? Be okay?

Look, I'm wobbling here. This sucks.

Ohgod, my voice is way too loud for being alone in the room. I mean, not alone, but . . .

I'm not going to be all weepy and pathetic if there's a chance that any of this is seeping in.

Hey. I think this is as close as I'm supposed to get.

That's Trisha at the door, giving me the hand waggle. I'm showing her one sec with my finger, so I've only got a minute.

Claire? I'm dragging a chair over, see? So I can be right next to you. I'm going to perform an act of supreme defiance. I'm going to—

That's me, touching your hand. *Ew*. It feels like a balloon kept in the freezer. But I love you so much I'll keep my fingers resting there.

I feel like . . . I want to . . .

Okay, whoops, out of the chair. Trisha's waving again.

I'll be back, okay?

Mwa. I'm going.

Fluids

Something I didn't want to mention to Claire is that she seems to have gained about twenty pounds overnight. And it's not just because she's bald so her face looks rounder. She is puffed up like someone stuck a bicycle pump in her ear and pumped fast.

When I ask at the nurses' station, they say it's the fluids. The patient takes in massive amounts intravenously, too much for the veins to hold; the spaces *outside* the veins get soaked. The cells and tissues absorb the fluids—especially the saline solution—and swell up. Claire is now a giant bloated sponge.

Fluids ranks right up there with *moist* on the Ten Worst Words list.

No Cell Phones Allowed in the Hospital

I go outside, onto the circular driveway that leads wrecked bodies to Emergency. I start to text Audrey but then I just call her.

"Nat?" she says. I might have woken her.

"Nat?" She has to ask twice because now's the moment I can't make a sound. Now's the moment there's a massive wave of heat and sorrow pressing up from my throat and inside my ears and behind my eyes, like lava. I'm deaf with it and blind and mute. Audrey hears me not able to speak.

"Do you need me to come somewhere?" she says. I shake my head, but she can't see. I press End and sink onto the grass. But only for about a minute because it's damp with dew, or maybe they watered already. I stand up, letting the tide ebb. I text Audrey, *later*, and I go back in.

Do Unto Others

I'm sitting in the waiting room and Janet Fox sits down beside me.

"Hello, Natalie," she says. "You've been in to see your sister? How did you find her?"

I could make a joke—I just looked in her room and there she was—but I don't. I want to say, It's the scariest thing I ever saw in my life, but I don't.

"Do you have any questions you'd like to ask?"

"Nuh-uh," I say, not meaning to be rude, but still, you know, wanting her to butt out.

"It must be . . . a confusing time . . . ?"

She's nice and everything, but I think I'm on my father's side as far as social workers go. How are we supposed to suddenly tell stuff to strangers?

"Oh, except . . ." I've thought of something.

"Yes?"

"It looks . . . She looks . . . I mean, do people ever . . . Is there any chance?"

"Oh dear," says Janet Fox. "That's one question I don't have the answer for. I can arrange for you and your family to talk to the doctor today." She pats my hand.

I nod. But she's not going to say what I want to hear.

"If you need anything, there is always a social worker on call, either me or my colleague, Kim Chan. And the chaplain is available, if you'd prefer to see him. There's even a chapel, if that would be of comfort. You just let us know. The nurses can find me anytime."

I'm wishing Claire were here to witness this woman's body because it's so oddly breastular that we could laugh for days.

Parents Show Up

I want enough time to pass so Trisha will give me another five minutes or else finish her shift. I'm reading the only magazine on the rack, called *Your Body, Your Health*, when Mom and Dad come flying in.

They are all weirded out that I came by myself while they were napping, as if I'd be less traumatized with them standing beside me.

"Honey, are you all right?"

"Uh-huh."

"You don't sound all right."

"Mom, my sister is in a coma."

So she cries and I apologize and we sit around.

We take turns all afternoon. Five minutes each time with ten minutes in between each visit. Trisha leaves and there's a Nan and then there's a Florence. The nurses decide not to be in the way after they see we're following a routine.

It Occurs to Me

It's not so shocking now that I've been in a couple of times. I can look right at you and not want to barf.

I look at you and want to cry. It takes a bit of . . . of *peering* to find you in there, Claire. The main thing is how still . . . Even a person sleeping isn't this still.

There are a hundred questions I need to ask you, but you're not giving any answers. So. It's up to me.

I think this is the part in the movie where I tell you what I always should have told you but never could. But you already know I love you. And we've been okay as sisters, right? I mean, better than okay. You get pissy and superior sometimes, but hey. I forgive you. Mostly, I . . . I . . . think I'm lucky to have you.

Okay, that part's done. I'm supposed to be talking to you about memories. Trying to kick-start any wires floating around in there. So I was thinking about it, out there in the waiting room. Does that mean reenacting terrible Thanksgiving dinners, like when Gram found out that Uncle Mike has a boyfriend? Or reminding you of when you won the state champion Smart Show-off Teen contest? Oh god. That's weird to think about, eh? How much *knowledge* is somehow trapped in your . . . in your hard drive . . .

Or maybe just if you hear my voice? Which must be the one you know the best, the way I know yours. This is like when I was little, around four or five, and I had the trundle bed that we rolled out from under your big-girl bed every night, in the house on Winona Drive. And you'd tell me a story in the dark about the Explorer Sisters, ClaireDare and NatBrat. You, of course, were the hero, and I was the tagalong. Remember that? I'd fall off a cliff and you'd save me. Or I'd get lost at sea and you'd find me in your hot-air balloon. One time, though—and I've always remembered this, Claire—once, you let *me* be the one to spill honey all over the bad guys so they'd get eaten alive by fire ants.

Or else we played Tickle Torture. Remember that? Where you would lean over the edge of your mattress and tickle me and I had to lie perfectly still without making a sound? You tor*men*ted me!

Oh, time's up. Nurse Nan is beckoning. Oh, that you could see me rolling my eyes.

See you later.

The Rest of the World, However, Moves In

Three casseroles are waiting on the kitchen table when we get home from the hospital, and a banana loaf and a platter of cookies and a basket of grapes.

"Oh dear," says Mom. "It's like when someone dies." She says it so quietly, so *evenly*.

"They're being neighborly." My father rests his fingers

in the center of her back and reads the note attached to a tub of lasagna. *Our thoughts are with you, from the Flemings.*

I peek under the tinfoil on another pan and see chicken paprika. *"We are praying for you all,"* I read. "Can we freeze this stuff?"

"Let's eat first," says Dad.

"I'm not hungry," says Mom.

"How about a glass of wine?"

Mom shivers and sits at the table. We got take-out chicken Caesar wraps from It's a Wrap on the way home, but they're kind of drippy and nobody wants them. It feels too late to heat up the neighbor food. Mom is just parked beside Dad while I'm the one who finds space in the freezer.

Gina

There's a knock on the back door. It's Mom's friend, Gina, of course. A friend in need. She doesn't usually knock, but . . . it's a new world.

She hugs me before I can slide away.

"Hi, Natty-pie," she says. I like Gina, but from a distance. She had a baby who died from crib death about five years ago, her only child. It always gives me the creeps, that she has this tragedy lurking just below the surface, like something more might be expected of me.

"Hi," I say, thinking now's my chance to escape.

"Sit down," she says. "I'm here to give you all five-minute neck rubs and a dose of Rescue Remedy."

Dad seems to squirm along with me, but we submit. Gina is a professional masseuse. It's kind of awesome what two thumbs and a bunch of fingers can do.

Altered Ritual

The kitchen door opens and Uncle Mike comes in. Dad jumps up and I shout, "Mike!"

"Chickie!"

But then we freeze. The way he's been greeting us probably since I was born is that he grabs what he calls a Chickie Head under each arm and then he knocks them together and Claire and I scream and laugh and that's Hello, Uncle Mike.

So the moment turns into this lurch of anguish. I go over and butt my Chickie Head against his chest and he says, "Hey, there."

Telling My Friends

I finally get to go upstairs and turn on music and not look at Claire's side of the room. Audrey shows up and finds me hiding. "I heard," she says. "Everyone heard."

She doesn't mention the zombies in the kitchen. She stands there, awkward, and I realize she's been wondering what to say, even though every day of her life since she was seven she's been showing up and standing in the doorway of my room and never once considered what she'd say.

I look at her and shake my head. Her face puckers up like a little girl's and she starts to cry. She throws her arms around me and rubs her forehead into my shoulder. Her hair is broom straw in my mouth, dyed a hundred times.

We're not really huggers, so it's only for a second, just to say, Hey, the world is upside down.

"So," says Audrey.

"Really bad," I say. "Hard to even tell you, because how could you believe what can happen to a person in a few hours?"

"A few seconds," says Audrey. "Actually a few seconds."

"Yeah, but the few seconds didn't make her look like that. The seconds were the catalyst."

"Oh, Mr. Harrison would be proud," says Audrey. "All that chemistry pays off. *Catalyst.*"

"They shaved her head," I say.

"Totally?"

"Totally."

"Didn't she just spend, like, eighty dollars on a haircut for the prom?"

I actually laugh. "Uh-huh."

"And what else?" asks Audrey.

"Well, I guess she's on some kind of meds that blow her up. Her face is twice the size. Tubes all over."

"So what do they think? She's in a coma, right? But then what? People wake up, right? Is she going to be okay?"

"They don't know. They don't say anything. Not to me, anyway. My parents are a train wreck, in case you hadn't noticed, and I . . . I don't know. I feel like I need to talk to Claire, you know?"

"Wanna go out?"

"Out?"

"Just to get out. Walk around. Everybody wants to see you, but they're all freaked out and don't know what to do. The whole town is freaked out."

"Do you think . . . Is it, I dunno, disrespectful or anything? What do you think my parents . . . ?"

"Like you said, they're a train wreck. Come on, we'll go to the Ding-Dong."

"On your night off?"

"It'll be a distraction. It'll be a pleasure to have Fiona wait on me. Let's go."

So we go.

And it's the Twilight Zone.

They're all sitting in the back booth, Zack and Carson and Leila and this other girl Trina, who's a total anorexic in Zack's grade. Belly is chiseling the grease off the sides of the grill, and Fiona, who is old enough to be our mother and not quite as shapely as she thinks she is, she's flitting around in the Dork costume.

It's just another night at the Ding-Dong. But it's really

not. I'm looking at the diner as if I'm wearing my dad's glasses. It's all hypersharp and familiar, but I'm thinking, How can it be the same? The back of my neck goes hot. I shouldn't be here.

(My parents didn't seem to care, actually. They smiled at Audrey, and listened while she said how dreadful, how sorry, how sad. But then they just said, Yes, of course, Natalie, go on out, see your friends. They didn't even say be careful.)

Am I imagining that the place goes dead silent? Except the *ching-grr, ching-grr* of Belly's spatula.

Zack leaps to his feet and comes running over, lifts me up off the ground, like he's congratulating me instead of condoling. Is that a word, *condoling*?

"Oh Nat," he says. "Oh, Nat."

I can see he's heartbroken, the way Audrey is, nearly the way I am. I have this flash of, Is he upset about Claire or is he sad for me? But then I know it's the same thing. He cares about both of us, but I'm the one here.

So Zack is holding one hand and Audrey has the other, and we walk over to the table in this bizarre formation that would never have occurred twenty-four hours ago.

That girl Trina stands up as we arrive and she says "Ohmygod ohmygod" about six times and puts her hand in front of her mouth as if I'm some phantom food-bearing invader and then she leaves.

"Okay," I say. "That was awkward."

There's only room for four in a Ding-Dong booth, which is usually okay because Audrey's working, but now we have to squish in. I can see that Leila is nervous that I might be squished in with her, so I sit with Carson. Audrey and Zack sit across, pinning Leila in the corner. We're all finally settled and it's quiet again.

I breathe a heavy breath, lifting my shoulders to my ears and then whooshing it out. This is only the beginning; these are my best buds, this is where it should be easiest. But how do we start? How do we get to the part where I feel comfort from them?

Whose Idea Was Fireball?

Carson's got this older brother, Murray, who will buy alcohol for the underage crowd. So Carson is equipped with a bottle of cinnamon-flavored whiskey the size of a hydrant. Not normally my favorite activity, somehow it appeals to me tonight, to huddle behind the bandstand in Queen's Park. It's so hot we stick to each other. We take turns swigging Fireball and screaming curses to scare off any couples who might be thinking of hooking up anywhere within earshot. By *curses* I don't mean swearwords. By *curses* I mean salutes to our blaspheming ancestors, whose profanities were universally more creative than the F word.

"Thou wouldst betray me?" I holler. "Thou shalt receive a bulging sack of boils and plagues!"

"Hey!" yells Audrey. "You vile knave! You lack-brained ninny! You malignant, short-panted cur!"

"Those aren't curses, Audrey, those are insults. Come on."

"You greasy, horn-mad hedge-pig! Thou shalt suck rabbits ere I speak with thee again!"

"Much better!"

"Thou hast offended greatly! Eat maggot pie, you pribbling swine! Eat until thy belly ripens and thy breath kills!"

"Good one, Zack!"

We could go on all night, once we get started.

Jumping into the Queen's Park fountain does not leave the same elated aftertaste pool-hopping does. Zack walks home with me, both of us sopping and pushing our bikes because after the first time I have to puke from the saddle, the effort of riding is way beyond my ability.

monday

Monday Morning

I guess they've turned the ringer back on, because it's the phone that wakes me. I wonder where my own phone is, it's been so long since I used it. Somehow the whole subject of Claire is something I can't talk about on the phone. Maybe that's a truth about Tragedy that I didn't know until now. What we thought were momentous events before, stuff we could discuss for days, there's no comparison.

I get downstairs and it's the same scene as yesterday: zombies and coffee, and despite the growing number of food donations on every surface, no one seems to be eating anything. Nobody's going to work either, so there's none of that *rushed* thing going on. Quite the opposite.

"Leight Pharmacy called," says Mom. That's where

Claire was cashier this summer. "To say . . . they'll take her off the schedule."

"The police are sending someone over this morning," Dad tells me. "Can you lose the pajamas, please?"

"Do I have to speak to them?"

"No, darling," says Mom. "Just look respectable in the background."

I go back upstairs and put on clothes. Including Claire's black thing under my T-shirt.

Claire's Friends

The doorbell rings and I look at the clock. Not even nine. What am I doing up?

"Nat," says Kate. Her voice cracks. She hugs me and I let her. She looks as if someone punched her in the nose, that's how dark the circles are around her eyes. Kate's got this amazing hair, like she stole it from an old painting: boisterous auburn curls, more like *coils*. But today, her hair is pulled back tightly, making her face pale and sad. I open the door wider so she can come in.

I look out and see a crowd of teenagers on the lawn: Carli, Mark, Feinstein, Tony, Stella, Val.

The girls are crying and the boys are glum. What is it about boys and crying? I've cried a thousand times in my life, probably. Or more, since that's only three times a week for about six years. So have all the girls I know. But boys? Maybe if they've just lost the basketball game, they tear up. And they don't want you to see them, so it's embarrassing. Carson cried when he got a three-day suspension from school for lighting the towel dispenser on fire, but that was more about being afraid of his father. And Zack cried when his grandmother died. But he was nine.

Claire's friends are all staring at me. I feel this huge flashing sign above my head: *NOT AS COOL AS BIG SISTER*

I pick up the newspaper lying there and go inside.

"Oh god, Mrs. J," Kate is saying. "I . . . I . . ."

Mom hugs her. "You don't have to say anything," she says. "I know how hard this is for all you kids."

Suddenly Mom is a mom again, making Kate feel better. She's one of the moms other kids like, so it takes another kid, maybe, to make her sound normal.

"I went to the hospital to see her," says Kate. "But they wouldn't—"

"No, sweetie. It's family only at the moment."

I think about all the times Kate made Claire so mad, the way she needs to be the center of attention. Parents only care if a kid is polite to them. Parents never know about drama. I think, Who's in the spotlight now? but that's too ugly a thought to hold on to.

Work

I had the closing shift at the Y yesterday, but I didn't show up and I didn't phone in. So I call, and Stephanie at the desk says, "Ohmygod, Natalie, are you okay? We heard about your sister and it's just the most terrible thing, are you okay?"

"I guess," I say. "Under the circumstances."

"Wait," says Steph. "Big Doug wants to talk to you. He said if you called to get him no matter what."

"Okay," I say.

She patches me through.

"Douglas MacIntyre."

"Uh, hi, Doug? It's Natalie Johnson."

"Oh. Natalie."

Will I ever say my name again, I wonder, without hearing the other person pause and be disturbed?

"I'm sorry I missed my shift yesterday," I say.

"No, no, Natalie, we completely understand."

No, you don't.

"Beth covered for you, no problem, came right in as soon as we heard. You going to need a few more days?"

I don't know what to say. He's telling me I don't have to work, but what else am I going to do? I'm only allowed in to see Claire for a few minutes at a time. And my friends are all working, so it's not like I've got anyone to loaf with. But does it look bad if I go to work? Will they think I'm a heartless freak if I do my shifts with my sister lying in a coma? I still need the money, but doesn't that sound beyond selfish? But what if she's like this . . . what if it goes on . . . for, like, months?

"Natalie?"

"Uh, oh, hi—sorry, Doug. I'm here. I think maybe I kind of need to work. I need to be doing something. Is that okay? If I come in this afternoon and just stay on schedule?"

"Well, yes, of course, Natalie," he says.

"I mean, there might be a day here or there," I say, trying to keep the option open. "You know, if things change . . . but right now . . . I . . . it's good to be doing something. . . ."

"Not a problem, Natalie. See you this afternoon."

Who Was Driving?

I'm trying to concentrate on Frosted Flakes, but the headline in the newspaper is distracting me. The picture is Claire wearing her mortarboard and gown.

CRASH VICTIM
STILL COMATOSE

A popular high school graduate and top-scoring player for the Central High soccer team is in a coma, in critical condition, following an accident Saturday night. Pedestrian Claire Johnson, 18, was hit by a car and seriously injured. Medical personnel made efforts to save her life at the scene, and she was admitted to East General Hospital at 11:34 p.m., where she remains in intensive care.

The driver of the car, Ted Scott, 28, of nearby Trenton, sustained minor injuries.

Overview

I'm in the bathroom upstairs with my forehead pressed against the window, catching the minute's worth of cool glass before it warms to match my skin. Dad and his brother are in the backyard with half the lawn mowed. But now they're standing close together, Mike's arm around my father. Just standing there. I imagine my hand pulling back and smashing through the window, the jagged shards shredding my knuckles and ripping my wrist, scarlet blood pouring out, staining the lacy curtain. I imagine the surprised look on the men's faces if I did that.

What Do They Mean, Exactly?

Coach McCafferty is not one of the policemen, so it's all business, from what I can hear. Kind noises at the door and then into the living room for questions. I hear Dad's voice going up.

"You're telling me the driver was not at fault? You're telling me *Claire* was to blame? Have you spoken to this young man? Or are you suggesting—"

But Mom cuts in to stop him with words too calm and quiet for me to catch at the top of the stairs. How could Claire be to blame? She's in a coma and the driver isn't.

Dad starts again. "Let me get this straight . . ."

I know Mom is pulling on his arm, trying to make him listen, be still. That's all we need. To make some lawyer-messed-up case out of this.

I start to close my bedroom door, but then I change my mind. I tiptoe down the stairs to listen. But they're in the hall already, saying goodbyes. "We'll be in touch," says one of the policemen.

And they go. How could it possibly matter? Could any answer change anything?

Mrs. Flint

No one else is getting the phone, so I do, and I regret it within seconds.

Taylor got back from the cottage late last night, so she just heard about Claire. She's crying so hard she has to hang up. Then she calls again and hangs up again, and then her mother calls, but I pretend there's someone at the door and I hang up. Mrs. Flint is someone I cannot deal with.

No more than nine minutes later there *is* someone at the door, and it's Mrs. Witchy Flint holding a plate of brownies. Taylor, with her face all red and puffy, has stopped halfway up the walk, as if she's six again and shy, coming for a playdate. But I know, from all the times before, that really she's dreading whatever is about to come out of her mother's mouth.

"How's your mother?" says Mrs. Flint, holding on to the brownies. "My Taylor's been in a dreadful state since she learned the terrible news, and we can't stop thinking of dear Claire." She manages not to say it, but I can hear her thinking, Thank heavens it's not My Taylor.

"Uh, Mom is resting," I say.

"I always knew those summer parties . . . All week Taylor was begging us to come back into town for the weekend, kept telling us she was missing the best parties and her life would be ruined. . . . Well, can you imagine? If she'd been here, she might have been mowed down right alongside Claire!"

"Mmmm," I say. Taylor waves her hands at me, denouncing any connection to this woman, and then puts her hands over her eyes.

"She'll certainly be a little more willing to listen to her

mother's instincts from now on. Wouldn't you say? Once again, teen drinking—"

"Claire wasn't drinking, Mrs. Flint," I say. "And it wasn't a teenager driving. Nobody was drinking."

"Oh, I doubt that's true, Natalie. There's always something to hide in these situations."

I want to punch her. "Are those brownies for us?" I say. Or are you just holding them as bait so I'll have to listen to you?

She hands me the plate. "Tell your mother I'll stop by again. If there's anything we can do, just give us a dingle."

"Uh, thanks, Mrs. Flint."

"Claire was Taylor's oldest friend."

Taylor has crept closer, behind her mother.

"Was?" I say. "She's not dead."

They both wince. "Oh my god, Natalie! Don't say that!" cries Taylor.

"Taylor, dear," says her mother. "Let's get you home."

"Yes," I say. "It's upsetting for all of us."

I shut the door.

Invasion of the Well-Meaning

Mrs. Flint only happens to be first. Gina shows up with this huge bowl of strawberries. Maeve Benson, who runs the health-food store, arrives with a bag of organic lettuce and a tray of carob nut clusters. Kate comes back with her mother and a plate of warm scones. I'm getting used to people throwing their arms around me, but the kitchen seems to be inhabited by extra bodies all the time. My brain wants to flee, but somehow I end up sitting there while they talk, first about Claire and then recipes and how hot it is and then about the sticky topic of college. Mom starts to cry again.

"I should be calling the registrar," she says. "Letting them know."

"Don't worry," says Kate's mother. "I'll do that for you. Nothing is so urgent as saving your strength for Claire."

Claire has a name for this little crowd of women who have poured a thousand cups of tea at our table; she calls it Mommy's Coven. We have our covens too. Claire has Kate and Taylor and Carli. I've got Audrey and Leila—and even Zack. Mom has Gina and Maeve and Shelley.

"Nat," says Kate. She tilts her head to say, Upstairs? So I go with her, and when we get to our room, she turns to me and says, "Are you mad at me?"

Somehow it makes me feel better that she's thinking about herself. So I don't have to.

"Of course not," I say. "I'm just, you know, blown into a billion bits."

"Yeah," she says. "You must be." And she starts to cry.

I have this guilty twinge, knowing that really she does love Claire.

"I miss her so much!" she wails.

Even if she loves herself more.

Our Room

Mom makes our room the thing she flips out about. Flips. All. The. Way. Out.

I'm on the computer, talking with Audrey, who is so mad at Leila that everything is normal for a minute.

audball says: such a sneaky spoiled brat

gnatbite says: no kidding but we know all that

audball says: ive been saving tips for a month to get that skirt & she goes & buys 2!

"Natalie!" Mom's at the door. She steps in and looks around.

"Hi, Mom," I say. "What did the cops want?"

She looks at me as if she's deciding whether I can handle the news.

"What?"

"The driver says that Claire appeared out of nowhere. That she ran into the road." Her hand goes to her eyes.

"Mom, you don't think . . . ? No way," I say. "You put that evil thought out of your brain right now. It was an accident, through and through."

"It had to be." Mom sounds so weary.

"What do the cops think?"

"They're just asking questions. None of it will make a difference to Claire."

I turn back to the computer.

audball says: i am so gonna spill something on her 1st chance i get

audball says: chocolate milk AND ketchup AND gravy

I think Mom's gone, but then, "Natalie Johnson, this room is a sty."

I glance around. It *is* kind of trashed. All the drawers half open, clothes on floor, both beds unmade, all surfaces hidden under dishes and debris. But no more than usual.

"Meh," I say. "Most of it is Claire's."

Like an alien possession the way she goes from Stoned Dowdy Mother to Shrieking Harridan in the time it takes to click a mouse.

"Getawayfromthatscreenthisinstantandgetyourbutt towork.Don'tyouthinkweallhaveenoughtoworryaboutwith outturningintocompletepigs?Howdareyoubehavelikethis inyoursister'sroomthrowing*shit*allovertheplaceasifnothing matters.Nothingcouldmattermorethanyoulookingafter everythinguntilyoursistercomeshome!"

She actually says *butt* and *shit*. And she gropes her way out of the room exploding into tears, fingers grabbing the doorframe so she doesn't fall over.

The rims of my eyes are burning, fighting tears. How

can she pick on me now? How wrong is that? I'm suffering as much as she is! More, maybe, since she's got meds to supposedly numb her feelings. I'm suffering more than *Claire*, even, since she's unconscious! Can't Mom see that? *I'm* the one with the black hole in my universe.

Archeology

I kick the door closed, *bam!*
Then,
gnatbite says: g2g, momspaz
audball says: boo, k bye
I sign off and roll onto the floor.

I have to breathe a few times, let the furious buzz subside. I hear Mom leave for the hospital, still crackly-voiced, telling Dad she's going to see Claire before she picks up her sister, Jeanie, at the train.

I get distracted and examine things from the floor point of view for a while. Picture of neglect. Plenty of dust bunnies. Dust antelopes, actually. Can't see too far under the beds, with the heaps of kicked-aside clothing blocking the vista. Except there's my red sweatshirt, lost before the end of school. And Claire's excellent prom shoes, half a size too small for me.

I find the shin guard that Claire had to pay for because she didn't return it, and here's Joe-boy's Sixers T-shirt that Claire swore she'd keep forever.

I start tossing stuff into a pile on the rug. Eventually, as the pile gets higher, I'm forced to stand up. I start at the top, folding each thing and sticking it on Claire's bed or mine. Even as I'm realizing there are clothes here that Claire may never wear again. *Don't go there.* . . .

The black thingy has not yet left my body.

The room gets cleaner than it's been in weeks. I put Claire's clothes into her drawers and mine into mine. Overflow into the laundry hamper, dirty or not.

Empty water bottles . . . recycling. Chip bags, salsa jar with fungus, apple cores, orange peels, frosted donut wrappers . . . garbage.

I'm getting carried away, using tissues to *dust* the dresser, lifting the lotions and scents and replacing them exactly. I spray Vanilla Musk into the air and breathe in Claire with a catch in my throat. There are movie ticket stubs, receipts from Beanie's, a few quarters, hair elastics, feathers collected on the beach at the lake. There are a dozen photos stuck in the frame of her mirror, scribbled notes, old birthday cards, the fortunes from about twenty cookies taped to the glass.

A lifetime friend shall soon be made.

A show of confidence can be as good as the real thing.

Alas, the onion you are eating is someone else's water lily.

I scoop her hoop earrings into the music box that tinkles a bar of "You Are My Sunshine" before I moan and slam it shut.

Life with Claire surrounds me, whichever way I turn. Every object has its own little story.

Graduation Present

Right in the middle of Claire's desk is her new computer. Uncle Denny and Aunt Jeanie pitched in to buy a laptop for her to take to college, since the TV-sized hulk we have in our room is not going anywhere without a team of mules. I almost cried with jealousy when her new one came: a baby Mac so sleek and silvery it begs to be stroked.

I have this icy hot rush from my temples on down. It's going to be mine now. And then I slap my own mouth in case I said it out loud, and the tears gush out like scalding tea.

How could I think such a thing? My sister's not dead and here I am looking at her prize possession, licking my lips. How sick is that? I cram her pillow against my face and scream into it. I'm sorry, Claire! I'm sorry! Ohgod, sorry, sorry!

New Scenery in a Small Town

I glance at Dad as we're driving along. He thinks he looks younger when he doesn't shave for a day or two, but he doesn't realize the whiskers are coming in silver. I reach over and pat his shoulder. He looks at me and winks. I suddenly realize where we are.

"Why did we come this way?" I ask him. "Look."

He slows down so we can peer over at the stuff piled on the lawn in front of the Dietrich Insurance building. I knew it was here because Zack has already been and read all the notes. It's like a garage sale spread out to tempt the passersby. There are bouquets of flowers lying there in paper cones. A sign lettered in glitter says CLAIRE. The hydrant sticks up like the Virgin Mary at a roadside shrine, surrounded by teddy bears and Mylar balloons and letters and candles and garlands. . . .

"Wow."

Dad picks up speed. "So, that's the spot."

He drops me off in front of the hospital.

"I'll be there in a bit," he says, and drives away. He's going to tell his client in person that the walnut case with beveled glass doors will be late.

Washing Her Feet

Mom's not here and the nurse is washing Claire when I get inside the hospital. It's Florence, the older lady, dark skin with springy white hair. She wears photos of her grandchildren in a locket around her neck. She's got a basin and cloths and she's giving Claire what she calls a sponge bath, without a sponge in sight.

"Hello, dear," she says. "How are we today?"

"Well, okay, I guess, you know."

"It's a tough thing to get used to, isn't it?"

"Um-hmm."

"You want to help me out? You could give your sister's feet a little massage. Keep the circulation going."

I don't expect disgust, but it jabs me like an elbow.

"Uh, I, that's okay, I . . ."

I don't like touching her, my own sister. Except of course she's not really Claire. She's changed shape, like in a science-fiction movie. She's swollen and pale and clammy-looking, as if her skin might peel back and reveal a subterranean insect tribe scuttling back and forth along her muscle fibers. . . .

Oh god, that's hideous. Why does my brain take me places like that?

"Come on over here, dear. There's nothing to be afraid of. Think how nice it'll be for her to have a little foot rub."

"Will she know?"

"It's nice to think she knows, isn't it? Put out your hands, I'll give you some lotion. That'll do the trick."

What choice do I have? Obey? Or run from the room and let them all know I'm a sissy who can't face her own sister?

Florence untucks the sheet at the end of the bed and

reveals Claire's feet. They look a little puffy, like the rest of her, but they're just feet. I can see that.

Florence says, "You all right from here? I've got other patients needing washing."

"Yes," I say. "I'm all right."

Your Feet

They're just your feet, after all. Okay, I've never given you a foot massage, but I've painted your toenails about a hundred times. Hospital lotion is unscented. What's the point of that?

I know your feet. Your second toes are longer than the big toes and you claim that's significant, that it means you're a descendant of Egyptian royalty, that it makes you a faster runner.

I know this jagged white scar on the side of the sole, where you stepped on broken glass on the beach at Lake Huron. We had to drive to the hospital in Bayfield with you lying on the backseat holding your leg up in the air so the blood would supposedly stop flowing so hard. You screamed every time the car joggled you, even if an insect hit the windshield. And I was squeezed over to my side because even though Mom wrapped the cut with picnic napkins, blood was dribbling down and you purposely kept swerving your leg in my direction, trying to gross me out. When we turned into the hospital parking lot, your foot hit me in the face and splattered blood over my lips and chin. At the Emergency reception they thought for a second that I was the victim. You straightened them out fast. And you got stitches. Eight or nine, I think. A lot, for a little kid's foot.

Must have been a beer bottle smashed to bits. Thoughtless teenagers, probably, Mom said.

On the way home, we both got Fudgsicles even though you complained that I wasn't hurt. Dad settled it by promising that when I inevitably did get hurt in the future, you could have one too.

So, you still have the scar, in case you were wondering. I guess they took off the nail polish. I've heard they have to do that in a hospital. They need to see your nails when they put you under so they can monitor your oxygen levels or something, during an operation. Goodbye, Ruby Champagne.

Okay, how was that? You now have the softest, most relaxed feet in town.

Word I Never Thought I'd Use About Claire

Flabby.

Medical Update

Dr. Hazel is the big star around here. He's more like a TV doctor than geeky Dr. Cooper: dark hair with silver threads, brown eyes that pay attention. The nurses flurry when he's expected or when he's in the corridor, with other doctors trailing.

So when Dad steps into his path today and says, "Hey, I'd like a word with you," I can see the flank guards ready to drag him down. Mom went to pick up Aunt Jeanie, so she's not here to interfere.

But Dr. Hazel looks at Dad and he stops his sailing doctor-walk and puts on that special face for families. He ushers us quickly away from the nurses' station, into a little office with only one chair. So we stand, too close together. I'm sweating and I keep my arms pressed down, hoping I don't stink.

"Mr. Johnson," he says. "And?"

"Natalie."

"Yes, Natalie. I know this is a difficult time for you."

"What can you tell us, Dr. Hazel?" Dad is fidgety, abrupt.

"We've been watching Claire very carefully," he says. "And performing ongoing physical examinations. What we'd like to see is a response to any one of several tests that would indicate some cognitive function."

"And?" says Dad.

It's way too hot in here.

"So far there's nothing."

Nothing. He said "Nothing."

"*Nothing?* But, that doesn't necessarily mean . . . You can't just say that's it, right? That she's a . . . a *vegetable*?" says Dad. "I've been doing some reading about this. . . ."

Dr. Hazel sighs. Not out loud, but his eyes sort of click out of focus, like *they're* sighing.

"There are plenty of cases," Dad goes on, "where the medical guys say there's no chance, but the patient somehow wakes up after a prolonged period of time and turns out to be okay. There was this one case I found on the Internet, about a man in Jacksonville, Florida, and he–"

"Dad," I say.

"His family never gave up," says Dad. "They talked to him and they prayed and they–"

Dr. Hazel pulls a pen out of the chest pocket of his white coat. He makes a note on his clipboard and then just taps the pen a few times till Dad pauses.

"None of us can discount what seem like miracles," the doctor says. "But they are very, *very* rare. The more time that goes by without reaction, the more . . . the likelihood of recovery diminishes."

"If she gets transferred to a bigger hospital?" says Dad. "Where they have more equipment?"

"Claire is getting the best possible care right where she is, Mr. Johnson. I promise you that. After surgery there's often a waiting period before we can assess how the body adjusts. We let the sedative subside and keep watching for . . . some sort of response to stimulation. At this point, we're about, oh, roughly thirty-six hours after surgery?"

"You would know," says Dad in a voice tight with, I'd say tight with *agony*.

"Yes," says Dr. Hazel, glancing at his gold watch. "We'll take a look at Claire again tomorrow morning, and likely schedule an EEG first thing Wednesday. Until then, get rest if you can."

I step backward out of his way, opening the door, knowing he's done. He nods to me, flashing some brown-eyed pity, and goes away. Dad's head is bowed, and he just stands there.

"Come on, Dad." I slide my hand into his and give him a tug.

"I need a minute."

"Okay," I say. "I'll go find Mom. I'll be right back."

Did You Ever See Dad Cry?

Okay, Claire, I'm going to tell you the saddest thing.

Dad and I talked to Dr. Hazel and then I went to find Mom. She wasn't in your room and I checked the lobby. Aunt Jeanie's train was late, maybe. I went back up to the fifth floor and I could see Dad in the lounge reserved for freaked-out families. It's separate from the regular place; the sofas are fabric instead of vinyl, and there are table lamps with cheesy maroon shades instead of fluorescent lighting.

When I look down the hall and through the glass door,

it's like seeing Dad through a spyglass, this hunched-over man, waiting for the next blow to fall.

I slide down next to him on the nasty brown tweed and bump shoulders, letting him know I'm there.

He doesn't say anything. But then he shudders and spits out this deep, gargling sob. His face squints up and his eyes are squeezed shut, so only the tiniest trickle leaks out. It's as if his tears have never been called on and there's nothing in there. It looks painful, and he's making this bleating noise.

I twist around and try to hug him. He grabs on and throws his whole shaking weight against me, like I'm the only hope. The *only* hope. My shirt rides up in back and the scratchy upholstery is scraping my skin. Tears swamp my eyes. Dad's clinging to me, and it's the most wretched thing that has ever happened.

Since the . . . accident . . . I haven't really . . . *looked* at him. I haven't ignored him, exactly, but he's been busy looking up cures online and hovering over Mom and figuring out who to blame and if there's anybody to sue and I just haven't paid attention.

But now he's not letting go; he's heaving and holding me tighter and tighter so I can't breathe. I've stopped crying, but how am I supposed to pull away? If a boy did this to me I'd scream, Get the hell off me, you freaking skeeze, but it's my dad and it's getting scary.

He's lost his mind. Bawling, out of control.

What if he actually *has* lost his mind? What if this is it? I'm witnessing the total collapse of a normal man.

The door opens and the nurse, Florence, comes in. She notices us and tips her head. But what is she actually seeing? Maybe nothing is a surprise in the distressed families lounge.

"Help." It's just a croak, but she hears me. She calls to someone in the hallway and then slides in, quiet on those heinous puffy white shoes.

"Honey," she says, touching my head.

And then she settles her nurse's hands on Dad's shoulders, reminders of civilization, of how fathers are supposed to be no matter what. Dad gulps, pulling in breaths like a little kid recovering. My mind repeats that word, *recovering*. Like a little kid *recovering* from a bike bump or a stubbed toe—and then I hear another thought.

There will be no recovery.

We are broken. Even fathers break.

It started with you, Claire, the one broken person. But there is never only one broken person.

Aunt Jeanie

"Natalie!" Aunt Jeanie hurls herself at me, squeezing my breath away.

"Un Jee," I say, my greeting muffled with my mouth crammed into her burgundy shoulder pad, bugging my eyes at Mom.

"How *are* you, baby?" Jeanie cups my face in her hands, trying to peer into my soul. "This is a big, hard punch, Natalie. There's no hiding from this one."

"Uh–"

"Jeanie, don't start," says Mom. Her little sister can drive her from mild to exasperated to insane in seconds.

"What we have to do is to share our strength and punch back! If we visualize Claire standing on her feet again, we can make it happen! Am I right?"

"Uh-huh," I say. Aunt Jeanie's voice is way too loud. She's bigger and rounder than my mother, even though she's younger. She's jollier too, except right now jolly is so wrong.

"Mom? Dad's in there." I point to the lounge, where he's sipping a Coke and gripping an ice cube in his fist.

"You take me to see Claire," says Aunt Jeanie, propelling me along the corridor. "We'll tell her that we're all pulling for her, eh?"

Wishful Thinking

I'm not sure what Aunt Jeanie was expecting, but it wasn't anything like this. I can only see her eyes above the mask, but they go wet and afraid as all her positive thinking melts into the humming quiet of Claire's room. I notice I have a stomachache from hoping she was right all along.

How We Make Room for New Truths

You don't look quite so bad today, actually.

It's scary how a person adjusts to being able to say that. To being able to *see* that. Because you're lying in a hospital with tubes crawling in and out of your body like garter snakes, but you don't look quite as . . . *bad* as you did yesterday. The bruises on your face are fading, sort of. To yellow.

It makes me think about that time we went tobogganing with Leah and Ben Skipton before they moved to Texas. When we had that colossal smash-up at the bottom of Kill Hill. We didn't tell Mom and Dad about it because it was hard enough getting permission to go with those older kids. And your whole arm was purple with bruises from being slammed underneath. You wore long sleeves for the first couple of days and it was winter, so no big deal.

But then we were supposed to be having a bath and your arm was yellow. Mom called out, "Get ready, spit-spot," the way Mary Poppins does. I dove into the art box and pulled out the finger paints and we slathered ourselves with green, yellow, blue, pink. And then we climbed into the bath. Mom had a complete fit. But with all the muck in the tub and on our skin, well, she never saw the bruising at all. Remember that?

I guess not.

I depended on you. . . . You're older, you're supposed

to be my . . . my *archive*. That's what sisters do, remember for each other.

But the cold, hard, horrible truth is that I don't feel you here.

Some of What the Principal Said at Claire's Graduation

"You'll have some tough choices in the years ahead— whether to continue your education, whether to travel, whether to join the workforce, start a family, buy a house. . . . But you will face some even harder choices— whether to socialize with people who drink and smoke cigarettes and marijuana; whether to stand up for someone who is being mistreated, at the risk of your own comfort; whether to tell a difficult truth or to rest with a simple untruth; whether to accept who you are or to change who you are. . . .

"Each of these dilemmas presents a challenge that I feel confident this class is prepared to meet. It is with great pride that I send you forth into the world. . . ."

A Couple of Things That Only I Know About Claire

The exact nanosecond her eyes will find mine when Mom starts to sing.

That she hooked up with Kate's cousin when she went to Kate's cottage even though she was with Joe-boy and even though Kate would kill her if she knew.

A Couple of Things That Only Claire Knows About Me

The day I got my first period, which I didn't tell Mom about till three months later.

How I really feel about Zack. Something Audrey may never, ever know.

I Like to Be the One Who Locks Up

I tell Shannon to go ahead, I'll close the pool by myself. She sticks around long enough to help drag out the lane dividers, but I do the rest.

I top up the chlorine tank and test the water chemical levels, which makes me feel like a scientist. I collect stray foam noodles, kickboards and life jackets and stash them away. I swab the decks with the squishy foam mop, muttering pirate curses the way I always do.

By the time I'm done the water's still again. There are always a few diving toys on the bottom of the pool, and those are my excuse.

I turn off the main lights, leaving the emergency pin

spots. I peel off my LIFEGUARD tank and shorts. I dive in, quick and sleek, being a penguin. It's my trick, getting in without moving the water. I go deep and roll over, gazing up at the surface. Is it called the surface when you're under it?

The lights gleam like stars through oil-slick shimmer; my breath bubbles upward in dancing crystal balls. Only underwater is a person so aware of the beauty of breathing.

Who Was Driving?

"I know the guy," says Leila. "The driver."

"You do?" I say.

"You do not." Carson thinks she's full of it, the way she always knows everybody.

"Yes, actually. He's a young guy, Ted something, only a few years older than us, like, mid-twenties."

"That was in the paper," says Carson.

"Ted Scott," says Leila. "And he works at that place out on Carlisle Street, where they rent equipment like backhoes and chain saws, for fixer-uppers."

"How the hell would you know a guy like that, Leila? Your addiction to heavy machinery?"

"Carson, eff off," says Leila, which is pretty strong language for her. "His wife works for my mother at the bank. I'm just telling you. Maybe Natalie needs to know he was a person too."

"I don't think I need to know that," I say.

"Yeah, right," says Carson. "A person who was wack enough to destroy her life in a split second."

"He wasn't wack," says Leila. "If anything, he was happy. His wife—"

"I really don't think I want to know this." He's the villain.

"His wife had a baby," she tells us. "On Saturday. She's still in the hospital. It's a little girl. Brianna Marie."

"No." I plug my ears.

The End of the World

Audrey is folding the paper napkins, making rabbits with stiff little ears.

"Thing is," she says, "we're in this whirlpool. Since nine-eleven we've been churning around, waiting for the world to collapse."

We all glance at Leila and observe a moment's silence because her father's cousin's new wife died on the ninety-second floor. Even though Leila had only met her at the wedding and no one was sure the cousin had made a good choice, this was the closest we came.

"But now," says Audrey, "to continue the whirlpool metaphor, we've been sucked against the drain with a crash. We thought the world would end but that we'd get off easy. Like, we'd be immolated in a fraction of a second, and it was sad and scary, thinking about it ahead of time, but the actual event would just, you know, be the end."

"Oh," I say. "You mean Claire's the drain."

"Well . . . ," says Audrey, ". . . yeah. I guess."

"There were plenty of times in history when they thought the world was going to end," says Zack. "Like the Crusades, for instance. How about if you were sixteen in 1091 and this thundering cloud of horsemen pounded through the village wearing metal body suits and not having washed for maybe a decade. And they raped you and they stole your father's grain store and then they raped your mother and burned everything else. And they said they were doing God's business. Wouldn't that seem like the end of the world?"

"Or how about the Plague?" says Leila. "That was nasty."

"It wasn't a healthy time in general," says Zack. "Aside from the Plague, there was plenty of consumption going around, and grippe and dropsy and fevers and rickets and rotting teeth! No one died of old age."

"I vote for the Nazis," says Carson. "Best all-time world-enders. Thought-out evil. Kind of brilliant, really. Organized death camps all over Europe, nothing but horror from the first roundup to the cattle-car trains to the bug-infested dorms to the gas—"

"Zyklon-B," says Zack.

"Yeah," says Carson, "With the gas gassing them in piles and then the pits full of bodies . . ."

"Did you know that Anne Frank has her own Dewey decimal number?" says Zack.

"Please tell me you don't know what it is," says Audrey.

"Nine four oh point five three four nine two," says Zack.

"Weapons are worse now," says Leila. "Push a button and blow up a whole city. Fly one airplane into a building and kill thousands of people."

"Two airplanes," says Carson.

"Are weapons worse," I say, "or better? Would you rather die, *pfff*, from a nuclear bomb? Or have your throat slit with a not-real-sharp sword? Or, god, like all those children in Africa, who had their hands cut off. How sick is that?"

"The thing that scares me the most," says Leila, "is that the Plague will come back. Sores or pox all over your face. Or other, you know, private places."

"The Plague has come back," I point out. "It's called AIDS."

"That's why sex is a bad idea." This is Leila's mantra.

"You don't have to have sex to die from the West Nile virus," says Zack. "Just get a mosquito bite. Or eat a burger and get E. coli. Or breathe and get SARS. Bird flu. Whatever. There are going to be about fifteen plagues that end the world, and every one of them will be really ugly."

"What if the terrorists have biological weapons?" says Leila.

"Won't be long, Leila." Zack loves to torment her. "If I were an evil genius, nothing would be more satisfying than infecting my enemies with smallpox or something that would cause festering boils, running pus and hideous pain."

"Good thing you're not a genius," says Carson.

Zack hits him. "But—Nat's question. Would you rather feel blinding, scorching pain and then die quickly? Or no pain, but prolonged, trembling decay instead?"

"My point," says Audrey, "was Claire."

"Oh yeah." They're all nodding, being sensitive.

"Claire doesn't have a choice," I say.

"Exactly," says Audrey. "She got it both ways."

"She's not dead," I whisper.

But what if she dies?

And what if she doesn't?

Joe-Boy

This day is longer than a week. I'm on my bike in the dark; my light's busted. It's maybe midnight and I'm pedaling back and forth outside Joe-boy's house on George Crescent. It's too late to knock. But I want to know what happened.

Someone said he went to the hospital, but they're still not letting anyone in except family. Dad went over to his house to talk to him, but I guess Joe was a mess; the police had been there. His parents let him stay in his room and gave Dad a whiskey. Dad was pissed off and told them he had a right to know what happened. But he still came home without seeing Joe.

I look in my phone and I've got his number.

I text him, *come down*.

I see his head silhouetted upstairs, looking out.

I wave. He disappears, without a signal. Is he coming, or what?

Why did this happen only to Claire and not to Joe? Did he jump out of the way? Did he try to save her?

Did she break up with him?

I hear the side door open, so I ride up the driveway.

"Nat?"

"Hey, Joe."

"How are you?"

"Oh, you know," I say. "Bad. How about you?"

"Really bad."

I'm glad they don't have one of those lights, like we do, that pop on when a raccoon goes by. A raccoon or a skulking teenager.

"I'm so messed up," says Joe. "I keep thinking someone is going to shake me awake and tell me it was a nightmare. It's just so, just so . . ."

And here's another reason boys cry: their girlfriends get hit by cars. Joe covers his face. I don't want to watch him, so

I go to lean my bike against the wall, but it sways and twists and knocks into him while he's trying to pull it together.

Then I lunge to catch the bike but Joe misunderstands and thinks I'm trying to embrace him. We end up standing there in this wrong hug, with the bike kind of pinned between us, and it's *so* awkward.

I step back and get the bike set. I sit down on the little step by the door.

"Have you seen her?" He sits next to me.

"Yeah."

He wants to know but he's afraid, I can tell. I'm waiting to ask him, but I'm afraid too.

"She's pretty bad," I say.

I think about today. I see her head and the gash and her swollen face and the tubes. I grope for the real Claire. The old Claire. I remember the prom photo taped to her mirror. Joe was her date, wearing a tuxedo, and they were so gorgeous it was ridiculous, like movie stars at a premiere. Now I can see her face, clear as clear. Her hair, darker than mine, cut so it would fall just right, no hokey updo for Claire.

"She was crying," says Joe. "She was telling me . . ." He stops, and when he talks again his voice cracks like a sad little kid's. "You can't tell anyone this. *Please*, don't tell. She was saying she thought we should, you know, spend the summer apart, because of going away in the fall. I couldn't even listen. I knew from the first sentence she was breaking

up with me, and I felt like my heart stopped. I got all . . .
well . . . I cried, Natalie. I cried. And then *she* started crying
and she tried to hug me and I told her to get lost and I
punched a telephone pole."

He holds out his knuckles, scraped and scabby. "See?
And then I turned around and said, 'I mean it! Get lost! I
don't want your pity! Don't be nice to me while you're
breaking up!' And I was sort of yelling but I was hiccuping
too, and that got me more pissed off. And Claire was crying so hard she must have . . . well, I guess she couldn't see
properly. And she went . . . stumbling back across the side-
walk and turned around to cross the street and then . . . oh
god . . ."

He has a hand over his eyes and he shudders.

"Did you . . . did you *push* her?" I say. "Is that why
she—"

"No! We were just, you know, mad, and . . . *emotional*.
But then this car came out of nowhere and . . . *boom!*" Joe
is whispering now. "Except it wasn't a boom. . . . The
sound I remember was the brake grinding, like *eeeeee* . . .
and a thud. A hollow thud. I keep hearing it, I keep trying
to figure out what it sounded like. . . ."

"Like a body," I say.

Joe moans. It's miserable. Animal in pain.

A light snaps on inside.

"Oh Nat." He grabs my arm and yanks me off the steps,
around the corner of the house. "Ssssh! My mom—"

We're in the dark near the garage. I can feel loops of hose on the wall next to me. Joe is leaning against the bricks, trying to recover his composure. The door opens.

"Hello?" calls Mrs. Russell. "Is someone there?"

Joe puts a hand over my mouth, but I twist away.

"What?"

"My parents said not to talk to you, or *anyone*," he whispers. "Your dad scared them, like . . . I *did* it."

My hand is gripping what turns out to be his bicep.

Claire had sex with him. That's what goes through my head while we're hiding there. The screen door bangs shut.

"*Did* you do it, Joey?"

"What? How can you say that?" His eyes are horrified.

"Because Claire is really messed up!" I yell. "She's really damaged! And you were with her when it happened! Why didn't you stop her? Why didn't you save her?"

I wrench myself away from him and grab my bike. I look back and he's standing with his tanned arms just hanging there. I hurtle down the drive, blind with tears. I scrape against the curb and grind my ankle so it rips and bleeds.

What Should Have Happened

Claire comes in and I look at the clock.

"Late." But then I see she's red-eyed. "What?" I say. "You did it?"

She plonks down onto her bed and nods, grim and un-happy while she takes off her sneakers. Then she says, "But you know what? He acted like a jerk, like a baby high school jerk. He cried and he punched the telephone pole and he was a pathetic idiot, so it just makes me know that I did the right thing."

"Poor Joe-boy," I say.

"Don't even start," says Claire. She throws a shoe at me, but she misses and topples my bottle of water, which spills all over my duvet.

"Aaah! Claire! You whore! Look what you did!"

"Oh, shake it out. It hasn't even soaked in yet!"

So I pick up my duvet and thwack it a couple of times like an oversized dish towel, and water sprays around the room and we laugh.

"Ice cream?" I say.

"And *Breakfast at Tiffany's*."

That's how it should have been.

Look at This

Dad's at the computer when I come in.

"Look at this," he says.

"I'm tired." I'm not going to tell him that I saw Joe-boy.

"Just for a second. Look at this," says Dad. "Your Aunt Jeanie told us about all kinds of times when people despair and then . . ."

So I go and look over his shoulder at the computer screen. He's got a list from Google of medical journal articles or maybe crappy tabloids, with titles like "Man with Head Injury Rewires Brain" and "Woman in Vegetative State Shows Signs of Awareness" and "Car Crash Victim Wakes After 20 Years in Coma."

"Dad." I put my hand gently on his plaid shoulder, pretending I'm the nurse. "Dad."

He slumps a little, hearing me through his hope.

But, "It could happen," he says. "We can't give up."

I sink into a chair. Have I given up? Or am I being realistic?

Sleep Has New Rules

Every part of me is aching and fuzzy, longing to be asleep. But when I get to my bed, my brain won't let go of this day. I want to lie on my side and whisper to Claire as if she's in the other bed, like all the nights of our life.

Maybe I can trick sleep if I try a different position. I stretch out on my stomach, pretending I'm on the beach. I lie on my back, being a vampire in a coffin with my arms crossed over my chest. I go back to my side and wait.

tuesday

First Sight in the Morning

Audrey is sleeping beside me like a puppy. How'd she sneak in? She's on the floor, not on my bed. And not on Claire's bed either.

I look at her face, her eyes crusted with black, lips parted and making a sound like there's a bug whirring in her throat. She's got a bath towel over her and she's curled up with her head on Claire's stuffed chimp, Finny.

I love Audrey, coming over here for me to wake up to.

I Step over Audrey and Go Downstairs

I don't have to work until noon but here I am at eight, as perky as can be, sitting with the ladies. The kitchen is already bustling, as if we're getting ready for a party and all hands are on deck. Aunt Jeanie is being hostess, pouring coffee, unwrapping more muffins from somebody.

Maeve went to high school with Mom. Shelley is Kate's mom, so she and Mom have been on school committees and all that. Gina's younger; Mom met her at the gym. They've been around as long as I can remember, but I haven't lingered in their company since my playground days.

"Can just you and me go see Claire?" I whisper to Mom. "Before I go to work?"

"Yes, darling, of course. But can we stop on the way? At Devon Road?" says Mom. "I think I'd like to see—"

I'm going to say no? It's the first time she's wanted to do anything, the first time she's spoken to me, really, since her wack attack in the bedroom.

I leave a Post-it on Audrey's sneaker: *ur the best.*

Dear Claire

Zack went yesterday and read all the cards and looked at the dolls and ribbons, and he said I should too, it might be good for me. Good for me? I wasn't going to, but then Mom . . .

We've been avoiding Devon Road on purpose, going around the other way to get to the hospital. It's as if some news channel is filming it, recording a tragedy with poignant details. We see it on TV all the time, whenever there's a heart-tugging victim. But now it's real life, our life,

where we can pick the stuff up and read it. We stand and
stare for a minute.

"But she's not dead," I say.

"It feels as if she's gone, though," says Mom. So she
knows too.

We swallow and go closer.

I pick up a folded card with a crayon picture on the
front of a big stick person and a little stick person, both
wearing triangle dresses.

> *Dear Claire.*
>
> *You are so prity. I hope you feel bet-*
> *ter. This is wen we went on a*
> *piknik.*
>
> *X O X O*
>
> *Michelle*

Claire looked after Michelle on Saturdays while her mom
went to business school. Try explaining this to a six-year-old.

> *Dear Claire,*
>
> *I was so saddened to hear of your*
> *accident. I know you're a fighter*
> *and if anyone can get back on her*

feet, it's you. My wife and son join
me in sending you the very best.

Coach Cop

Dear Claire,

You are the best friend I ever had
in my life and I can't believe this
happened to you.

I love you,

Taylor Flint

"Who's this?" Mom asks, handing me one.

Dear Claire,

It makes me feel really out of
control that bad things can happen
to such a nice person in a normal
place like this. Now I'm afraid all
the time. I hope a miracle happens
next.

Your friend,

Steve

"I don't know," I say. "There's a Steve in her class, but he's kind of—well, he plays chess, basically, so I don't know if this is him."

"If this is *he*," says Mom.

> *Dear Claire,*
>
> *Jesus Christ our Lord is waiting for you with open arms. There is nothing to fear. May your journey be painless.*
>
> *E.G.*

Sure, I think. Don't sign your name. Painless.

> *Dear Claire,*
>
> *I wish we had sex.*
>
> *Toony*

That one I crunch up and slide into my pocket while my mother is bawling her eyes out, touching teddy bears and miniature soccer balls.

"Can we go now?" I ask.

My mother puts down the card she just picked up. "Yes," she says. "I think I've seen enough."

She brings Michelle's drawing with her.

"Maybe we can pin up some of these in Claire's hospital room," she says. "To brighten the scenery."

Mom

When we arrive in the parking lot of the hospital, she turns off the ignition. I open my door and get a blast of heat from the real world. Mom's not moving, aside from shivering. I didn't notice that the car is freezing till I opened the door. But Mom is just sitting there, so I pull my feet back in and close the door and look at her.

If she's this stoned, I think, she shouldn't be driving. She's just staring out the window with her lower lip pushed slightly out, looking petulant. But then I guess, Oh, maybe she's afraid. To go back inside for another day.

"Natty," she says.

"Uh-huh."

"This is not the way it's supposed to be."

"No kidding."

"People tell me we'll be okay, but it's hard to believe, isn't it? I feel like I won't ever be okay again."

I look at her. "I know."

"I had these babies," she says. "These darling babies. And from the first second that I held a living creature in my arms, I was terrified. First Claire and then you. It was just the idea, in the beginning, that I was responsible, this little bug could live or die because of me."

"Mom."

"Look what happened to Gina! She put Alexander to bed one night and he just died. Crib death. Over. Oh my god, the way I paid attention to my babies . . . And then you went to school. And to parties and camp and playdates and movies and riding in other people's cars. Even other parents' cars. A part of me was unable to breathe or think until you were home again."

"That's a little extreme, isn't it?" But then I swallow. Nothing is extreme, it turns out. Anything can happen.

"So all this time I've been expecting the terrible phone call. . . . And then it came. You'd think, since I've been waiting forever, you'd think I would have made a plan for the next part. . . ." Her eyes start to tear. "Wouldn't she hate this, Natty? If she knew she was . . ."

"She would. She'd totally hate it."

"It's so . . . I can't bear . . . to see her this way."

"I know, Mom."

"And you're my baby too." She smacks the steering wheel. "But . . . how can I ever be a whole mother again?"

I lean over as far as I can in the car and try to hug her. She leans against me. She laughs just a little while she's crying because it's so clumsy.

"I love you, Mommy."

It slips out and makes her cry more but I'm glad I've said it.

Okay, Shoot Me

What is the deal with old women and facial hair? I know it's some function of aging and not producing estrogen and blah blah blah, but these old dames at the hospital, they've all got nasty spiky hairs growing out of their chinny-chin-chins!

One lady today, her name is Blanche, which I know because she's got it written in BLOCK letters on a giant sticker on her cardigan, *upside down,* so that when she forgets who she is, she tips her tag and reads her own name.

So Blanche is in a wheelchair in the hallway close to the intensive care unit. She's got a rolling IV apparatus and she's wearing slippers that without a doubt she knit herself, green-flecked woolies with pom-poms on the toes, like portable cat toys. She's clearly listening to music from an alien spaceship, because she's tapping her feet on the wheelchair footrests, and she's snapping her fingers and she's jutting out her hairy chin with the biggest grin on her face. Till she sees me.

"Hold your horses," she says.

"Hello, uh, Blanche," I say.

"You enduring?"

"Uh, yeah."

"You just cry if you need to," she says. "You deserve it. You are never going to be short on tears, from here till the end of time."

And I believe her. I have this vision of myself wearing Blanche's dressing gown and Blanche's slippers. I'm a distressed old crone and my heart is still breaking for Claire.

But you can be damn sure I'll be plucking out those chin hairs!

Last Times with Claire

Last fight: Well, the black thingy wasn't really a fight, but it feels like one now. It *would* have been, if she'd known.

Last movie watched—don't laugh: *The Princess Bride.* Our all-time favorite line: *My name is Inigo Montoya. You keeled my father. Prepare to die!*

Last purchase together: Flip-flops at the mall. Two for five dollars. I got green and she got bronze.

Last thing she said to me: Mwa.

The Mailman

Charlie's been delivering mail to our house since probably before I was born. His kid Ali goes to our school. His wave is usually the cheeriest of the day. But this week he's bringing a stack of envelopes so weighty he shakes his head and hands over Get Well cards like sheaves of thistles. He stands on the doorstep as if he needs to say something, but then he backs down the steps and goes off muttering his Jamaican oaths.

Mr. Dodd's Letter

Dear Mr. and Mrs. Johnson and Natalie,

It was with great sadness that I heard about Claire's tragic accident. As Claire's principal since the eighth grade, I have come to admire her good humor, her optimism and her resilience as an athlete. It is these qualities that I believe will carry her through to a full recovery. My wife and I, on behalf of the entire school community, extend our heartfelt good wishes to your family during this difficult time.

Sincerely,

Michael P. Dodd

My Bike's in the Back So I Can Use It Later

"Where are we going, Dad?" This is not the way to the Y. Then I read the street sign. Carlisle Street. *Uh-oh*. Dad pulls over in front of a garage-type building painted yellow. U-RENT-IT! U-DO-IT! says the sign. The big doors are open and there are giant machines and tools inside.

"Dad." I have this instant chill. Dad is just staring over there. I hear Carson's voice, And then the father, insane with grief and pumped up on revenge, he gets out of the car and it's a wide-angle shot, and you can see the crowbar in his hand. . . .

"Dad!"

"Do you think that's him, Natalie?" says Dad. His hands are holding the steering wheel and he's pointing with one raised finger.

"I don't know," I say. But I'm also kind of peering at this guy in shabby jeans and a muscle tee. He seems to be rubbing a rag over the blades of a lawn mower that's turned upside down in the drive.

"Keeping himself busy," says Dad.

"I think he was injured too."

"Not so's you'd notice."

"Maybe that's not him."

"Oh, that's him, all right. Just tinkering, going about his day. Like he's got a tomorrow."

Being a Lifeguard

I learned to swim at this same Y. I bet Mom and Dad did too. It's not some gleaming modern aquatic center, it's a moldy little old-fashioned pool-in-the-ground.

The first time I made it from the ladder to Mom's arms eight feet away, Claire was hopping up and down, yelling "Go, Nat, go! Go, Nat, go!" Everybody in the pool joined in and I doggy-paddled as if I were finishing a triathlon. I try to pass along that triumph to the Tadpoles, making them blow bubbles, get their faces wet.

Of course, mostly I just have to tell them the rules ten times per lesson.

"Hey, Milo," I say. "No running. You know better than that."

And he grins at me, that little-boy-with-one-tooth-missing grin, as in, If I flash my cutest smile you won't notice that I'm gonna run again the second you turn your lifeguard head.

And he does, only this time he slips on a wet patch and wipes out, *thwack,* skull to the tiles. The sound echoes like a bark and I'm blowing my whistle, *shreet shreet shreet,* before I even think about blowing my whistle.

The kids all know, I've drilled them; they're out of the pool and shivering on the side, gaping at Milo. And Milo, he's lying there like . . . ohgod, like Claire, still as stone. But before I get to him, before his mother's off the bleacher, he lets out a wail that's the sweetest sound I ever heard. Crying kids I can deal with. Breath-sucking silence I can't. Suddenly I'm infected with Responsibility: it's up to me. I'm guarding their lives, and anything can happen.

Zack

Zack meets me at the Y as a surprise.

"Yay, Zack."

"Audrey made red velvet cake." He takes my swim bag so I can fiddle with my bike lock. "Come over."

"I don't know." I'm afraid Zack might look me in the eye and expect someone to be there.

"Why are you working, anyway?"

"Routine," I say.

"But everything's different."

I unlock my bike. "It sure is."

"So?"

"It's hard to be at home. They're kind of . . . marooned by mourning." That phrase came to me beside the pool and now I'm saying it out loud.

"Aren't you?" he says.

The lock slips out of my hand and clanks on the ground. How can I still have a crush like a kid when the rest of me is . . . grappling with *real* stuff? "I am too."

"Audrey told me to bring you home." Zack picks up the

lock and hands it over. "But maybe you just want to go to the hospital."

"Yeah." I reach for my bag and cram it into my basket.

"What's it like?" he says. "I can't even . . ."

I notice we're almost whispering.

"I've been trying to imagine," he says. "If it was Audrey."

I shudder. "I keep thinking it's not true. I wake up and trick myself every time. Today it'll be all fixed. But it's still true."

"You okay?"

"Yeah, you know. I'm okay."

"What should I tell Audrey?"

"How about if I meet you guys later?"

But then.

"Zack."

And he turns back, eyebrows up.

"I'm faking," I whisper. "I'm not okay at all."

My bike is suddenly too heavy to hold and I lay it down.

Zack scoops his arms around me. Zack. Who knows not to say anything stupid. I'm smelling his ice-cream-sticky shirt and sort of pressing into him. In a way I never have before.

For one second I consider pulling back and making a joke. But I think, Anything can happen at any moment. What if a car leaps out at me and I've never kissed Zack?

And then I'm kissing him like crazy; hot and tongues, chlorine and vanilla. I'm gripping his new gardening shoulders and his T-shirt soft as tissue, washed a hundred times. His hands are cupping my face, and I feel . . . cherished. I like this skinny boy so much . . . but now I'm crying too, tears streaming, and the kiss turns salty, like we're bobbing in the ocean.

Of course it has to end. And here we are outside the Y, with traffic and a wasp and summer dust and each other's faces in a new light.

Whoa

"What just happened?" he says.

I laugh and sob together, unzip my bag and pull out the damp towel to hold over my face, my burning eyes.

"Nat?"

I shake my head, inhaling the pool.

"Nat, just so you know . . . I . . ."

I wait, still hiding.

"That was . . ." He tugs at the towel. He wraps his arms around me again. "You mad?"

I shake my head.

There's No One to Tell

Because I sure won't be saying anything to Audrey. And what's the point of telling Claire?

The Regulations Seem to Be Loosening

Mom and Dad are both in Claire's room, sitting side by side, holding ungloved hands and not wearing their masks. They're using both chairs, so I sit on the floor next to Mom, where she can rest her other hand on my head. I slide my own mask down. Maybe it'll be good luck if we're all breathing the same air.

Can You Imagine?

"Wouldn't it be the most awful feeling to hit someone with your car?" Leila can't let it go.

"Since I've decided I'm never going to drive," I say, "that's one experience I will definitely avoid."

"Amaxophobic," says Zack, "and stick with your instincts."

We look at him.

"Afraid of riding in cars."

"Does anyone notice how sick this conversation is?" Audrey asks. "Considering?"

I Can't Think About It

All night Zack is watching me, but I'm not letting my eye get caught. Finally he snags me alone outside the Ding-Dong ladies' room.

"Hey, Nat."

"Hey."

"Was I dreaming this afternoon?"

I laugh. "No."

"So?"

"I'm in kind of a weird zone, Zack."

"Well, yeah."

"So . . ."

"Just please don't say 'Let's pretend it never happened.' "

"I couldn't pretend that," I say, not wanting to grin under the circumstances, but knowing we sort of just shook hands on a deal. "But I can't think about this right now."

He leans over and I hold my breath. He touches his nose to my neck, so lightly.

"Whenever you can," he says.

Dream

I hate when people tell you their dreams, like they mean anything to anyone but the person who dreams them.

But I just dreamt about you. I dreamt that my cell

phone rang and the display said CLACK, like I used to call you. So I answered and you said "Hi, Natty" and my breath caught in my throat and in my dream I felt like my head would pop open.

"Claire!" I said, giddy with relief. "Claire! Everybody thinks you're dead."

And you laughed. "Well, here I am," you said. "Everybody's wrong, as usual."

And I was holding the phone, pressing it against my ear like I was breathing through it. "Where are you?" I said.

"I'm going to L.A." you said. "Get it? The City of Angels."

"Don't go," I said. "I need to talk."

But I couldn't hear anymore and I woke up with my hand hot against my ear.

My clock says 2:09 and I'm so awake I'm electric. I can't hear you breathing from the other bed. I look over and the duvet's bunched up but you're not there. You're really not there. It was a dream.

Visiting Hours

I feel like I have to see her now and not wait till morning. What if this is one of those cosmic moments where she's calling me in my dream but I go back to sleep and only think about it later when they tell me Time of Death, 2:09 a.m.?

I splash water on my face and put a cold, damp hand on the back of my neck to startle myself. I trade boxers for shorts and sneak out of the house, which is so easy I should do it more often. Dad snores and Mom's on drugs. The garage door makes that bent-metal screech, but really, who's going to wake up or care? I pat my bike like she's a pony, waiting for me in her stall.

At the hospital I avoid the main entrance. They probably won't let me in. I go through the Emergency door and sit in the waiting room while I figure it out.

There's a mother holding a little boy who is chalk faced and breathing weird. An old lady is clutching her purse, but I can't tell what's wrong, other than she needs a comb. There's a guy who is piss drunk, with a face somebody punched, his lip puffed up like a donut.

Only medical personnel are supposed to go through the swinging doors, but the nurse at reception is tapping away at her computer and not watching the room. So when the old lady gets everyone's attention by starting to cry, I slip through and head for the elevator.

On the fifth floor, intensive care, I expect Claire's room to be dark, but when I step into the scrub room I realize there's a light, and a nurse sitting inside next to the bed, knitting. I haven't seen this one before. She's older than the day nurses, gray hair cut short, as in hacked off with nail scissors to look like a molting mouse. I wonder what's she doing here. Should I leave? Do I hide and wait for her break? Do I just go in?

I wash my hands and put on the gown and the mask. I open the door and the nurse looks up.

"Oh," she says, "who are you?"

"I'm the sister. I mean, I'm Claire's sister. I'm Natalie."

"Hello, Natalie."

"I know it's not really visiting hours . . . but . . ."

She looks at her watch and laughs, "No, not really."

"But I really wanted to see her," I say. "I had a . . . I had a dream." That sounds lame. "I just wanted . . . Has anything changed? Is there any difference?"

Now that I'm looking at Claire, I think, How could there be any difference?

She shakes her head, feeling sorry for me, I bet. "No, dear."

"Do you think . . . I mean, you must have seen situations like this before," I say. "Lots of times . . . Is there ever any hope?"

She considers me for a moment. "Depends on what you're hoping for," she says.

Quiet.

I turn to look at Claire. What am I hoping for?

My heart hammers like when a wave knocks you head over heels. I know. What I've been hoping for is impossible.

Claire will never be Claire again. She might not even

open her eyes again, and she sure isn't going to go to college in the fall, or play soccer, or marry Joe-boy or anyone else. She won't ride a bike or pool-hop or scarf cookie dough or dance with me on our beds till we fall *ploof* onto the duvets. Her life took eighteen years to make and now it's over.

My life is over too, the one I had coming up right behind her, attached to her, sewn onto her even when I was swimming in the opposite direction.

What would Claire think? Would Claire like this? How would Claire do it? I don't care what Claire says! Claire, Claire, Claire . . . the only one who knows all the stuff about my life, the only witness.

This nurse seems to know what's careening through my head. She puts a cupped palm under my elbow and sits me down. I see her knitting tucked into a tote bag. Pale, fluffy, *hopeful* pink, tiny needles; must be for a baby. Someone just beginning.

I stare at Claire. She'd never, ever want to know that this is where she is. It's time to find something new to hope for.

wednesday

An Alternative

I wake up sweating with my arm trapped in a twisted sheet and I almost scream getting it out.

What if all this had happened to me instead of to Claire? What would Claire do?

Today's List

Things I'll Never Be
A nurse who dyes her hair a really bad color
A nurse of any kind
A ballet dancer
An astronaut
A driver
An aunt

Electroencephalogram

It's Dr. Hazel who tells us all the jazz about the EEG, aka *ee-leck-tro-N-ceph-A-low-gram*.

"It's a noninvasive procedure," he says. "To observe whether or not there is any activity in the brain. We attach electrodes to the scalp that will pick up any electric signals produced by the brain . . ."

Who can listen?

Why Medical School Takes Five Extra Years

So they can learn how to confuse patients with jargon and convoluted sentence structure.

Drama

I meet Audrey before she goes to work. She's unsnarling her hair, cursing and jabbing the comb like a machete. Zack is there and I tell them about Claire's EEG.

"The brain's electric?" says Audrey.

"Not the way you're thinking," says Zack. "It's not a toaster. It produces electrical signals, sort of like microscopic sparks. They use an EEG in this situation to detect whether . . . if Claire . . . if there's any flicker of action."

"That's pretty much what the doctor said," I say.

"Okay, you can disappear now, Brain Child." Audrey pushes him. "I need to speak to Nat."

"Can we see Claire?" says Zack.

"Uh, well, they say family only. But maybe."

Zack rubs my hair and leaves.

I ask Audrey, "So?"

She doesn't look at me, but suddenly she's smirking. *Uh-oh*, I think. Does she know about Zack and me?

"I had an inappropriate coupling," she says.

"A *coupling*?"

She doesn't know.

"Well, not actually, but partially."

"Who?" I ask.

"Don't laugh."

"I won't."

"Don't yell at me," she says.

"Oh crap, who was it, Audrey?"

She looks over her shoulder.

"How inappropriate can this have been?" I say. "I'm trying to think of the worst possible—"

"Carson."

"Carson?"

"Sssh!"

"You're joking, right?"

"See? I knew you'd be a butt about it."

"I'm not, wait, I'm not anything about it yet. I'm just trying to find out if you're telling me— Wait, *Carson*? The one we've known since junior kindergarten Carson? The one who wears tighty whiteys and farts when he eats hot dogs Carson? The one who says the wrong thing every time Carson? The one who—"

"Okay, Natalie, I think we both know which Carson we're talking about here."

"You *hooked UP* with him?"

She grins right at me.

"What? It was *good*?"

"He's the *best* kisser," says Audrey.

"So why are you in a crap mood?"

She remembers, and scowls. "He said it was a one-time only. He doesn't want to ruin our friendship."

"But—"

"I know, how dare he?"

And she stomps off.

There's always drama.

What's the point, otherwise?

After the EEG

I keep thinking how I'm so mad at you, only then of course I can't be mad at you, but I keep getting jolted with dark, steaming thoughts . . . like Why the hell did you stumble into the road, you idiot? How upset could you be, since *you* were the one breaking up with *him*? Why were you so deranged as to step in front of a car?

Another Visit

"These are my cousins," I say. "Audrey and Zachary."

Trisha looks them up and down, pausing to read Zack's T-shirt: HELL IS A STATE OF MIND.

"One visitor at a time," she says.

"Oh, please, Trisha! It's not like we're going to tire her out!"

"You bite your tongue, girl." But she makes a point of turning her back so we can file into the little scrub room.

"You've got to swipe me one of these gowns," says Audrey. "My bag's too small, but get me one, okay? I've got this idea, to turn it into—"

"Oh, and I want a hat," says Zack, tugging on the paper shower cap.

"Take it," I say. "All yours. Your very special souvenir from Claire World."

Zack checks my face to see if I'm being sarcastic, but I'm not. I know what they don't know. They're going to walk through the inner door onto another planet. Nothing will ever be the same.

Suited up all together with our masks on, we look like a team from a bio-horror flick. Good thing Carson's not here to comment.

We stand beside Claire's bed, speechless. For a long time.

Then, "Wow," Audrey whispers.

"Her hair," says Zack.

"Or not," says Audrey, and then slaps a hand to her mask. "Sorry."

They stand some more.

"We shouldn't be just *standing* here," says Zack.

"What do you do when you're here alone?" Audrey asks.

"I talk to her."

"Wow."

"The nurses say, you know, maybe she can hear. So I tell her stuff."

I move closer to the bed and stroke her hand. Her puffy, purply hand.

"Hey, Claire," I say. "You've got company."

Zack is next to me so close his chin is hooked over my shoulder. Audrey goes to the other side of the bed.

In the quiet the machine is like a heartbeat. Well, *bi-bip, bi-bip,* like a robot heartbeat.

"It's sort of holy, eh?" says Audrey. "Like we're in a cathedral and she's one of those stone crypt things, you know? Lady Claire."

"She's not dead," I say.

"Oh god, sorry. Sorry. But it's . . . so still. That beep is sort of like praying monks, you know? An incantation . . ."

Audrey begins to hum, this pure, melancholy note, and Zack jumps right in, lower, in harmony. I can't help it, I pick a note and join in. We start out solemn, chanting the way they do in recordings of medieval rituals. Then Zack introduces some bebop and Audrey starts snapping her fingers.

I'm swaying and the room is adding echoes while we Rip It Open for Claire.

Trisha's face at the door is horrified. We stop.

"This is intensive care," she says. "The recording studio is in the next block."

"Sorry," I say. "We were cheering her up. See? Isn't she smiling more than she was before?"

We all look at Claire, wishing.

Special Needs

They're supposed to have their swim from three to four on Wednesday afternoons, but they're never on time. Never. There's an instructor one on one, for each of the six kids in the pool. To hold them up. I'm only there to lifeguard, so staring is part of the job.

These are kids with serious "challenges," as we're supposed to call them. Cerebral palsy, muscular dystrophy; there's one boy with some kind of genetic situation, meaning he has hands like fairy wings coming out of his shoulders with no arms in between. His name is Eddie, that kid. He likes to float on his back and ripple the water with his fingertips. He's the only one who's not in a wheelchair outside the Y. He's got two working legs, but I watch him every week thinking, Would you rather have no legs or no arms?

I asked them that at the Ding-Dong one time and Carson said, "Easy. No legs. Then I could park in the handicapped spot."

"I think no arms qualifies too," said Audrey. "You're set, either way."

I sit watching these kids, wondering every time how it would feel to be so . . . so *knotted* in your own body. Accomplishing the day would seem so overwhelming. And some of them have fully equipped brains, even if they can't talk. So they know.

They come in today and my heart is in my throat, gagging me. I wave at Eddie and he waves at me, his little fluttery wave. He must be about eleven. I think about him being a teenager, about him hearing the other guys brag on unhooking girls' bras and knocking back beers. How's he ever going to knock back anything? He drinks through a straw. And girls? He can't even, you know, touch *himself,* let alone any girl who manages to love him without him being able to hug her. The image comes of Claire lying there in stone, forcing the tears up hot and fast, so I can't see for a second and I feel my nose go red.

"Natalie? You okay?" It's Brian, one of the caregivers.

"I don't feel well," I say. "I think I'm going to call Shannon back from her break." And I run out of there, banging on the office door, snot bubbling, telling Shannon I've got to leave right now.

The very, very, very best possibility for Claire would fall way short of these kids. What if she knew she'd never be underwater again? That's just— Oh, it's really better that she doesn't know.

Eavesdropping

I hear Aunt Jeanie on the phone and I'm not really listening, but then I'm suddenly, *bing*, alert.

"Well, you know, according to statistics, very few marriages survive the death of a child. . . ."

She's not dead. Who is Jeanie talking to? Does she think Mom and Dad are going to break up? Oh god. Does that mean she thinks Claire's going to die?

I need to talk about this. With Claire.

Will there ever be a day when I don't think of her? Will there ever be an hour?

And if there is, will it mean that I'm mature? Or that I'm a coward, and I've stuffed her away in a hiding place?

Which would I rather not be?

I've Been Trying to Put It Into Words

I feel as if I'm swollen. Swollen with sadness.

There Are No Words

Audrey's with me on my bed, snug like sisters. We're facing the wall instead of Claire's side of the room.

"I keep thinking," says Audrey. "About Joe."

"I know," I say.

"Don't you think he must feel like the worst human ever?"

"Yeah." I see his face, squeezed up and crying, his brown arms sticking out of his T-shirt, hands dangling, helpless.

"How do you ever get over something like that?" Audrey is playing with my hair.

"I don't think I'm the person—Ow! Audrey!"

Her fingers are caught in a tangle.

"Oh, sorry, Nat, sorry. . . ." She tries to comb out the knot with her nail, but it bugs me and I pull away. But not all the way away because I need her there.

We lie still.

"I don't know what to say," Audrey whispers after a while. "To you. Sometimes. About this."

Vote

I'm watching Audrey and Carson for signs of anything. There's nothing obvious except that he's not looking at her and she's not looking at him.

"What would you do?" I ask. "Not that it's up to me, but it's all I can think about. If you had to choose . . . would you rather just die, or be alive and seriously brain-damaged?"

Audrey opens her mouth but nothing comes out. The

others stare at the table. Leila gets that mottled pink flush on her cheeks.

"Die," whispers Zack. "I don't want to say it."

"Good," says Carson. "I was waiting for someone else to go first. I take die, for sure. No way do I want to be a cripple."

"Okay, Carson, stop now," says Audrey. She picks up a paper napkin and strips away the edge of it with her amethyst fingernails. "This feels kind of bigger than the game, Nat."

"Well, yeah," I say.

Another wisp of napkin floats down.

"Wait," says Leila. "What is the extent of the brain damage?"

"Bad," I say.

"Can I talk?" she asks. "Can I at least understand what people say to me?"

"We don't know yet," I say. "But how about 'to a certain extent.'"

"Then I choose brain damage," says Leila.

"You do?" I get this quiver that Leila knows something surprising or hopeful.

"It would give me the opportunity," she says, "to learn sign language."

"Christ," says Carson. "You're in a wheelchair with probably spastic arms. Your body is kind of twisted so you have to wear ugly clothes and you'll never have sex. I don't think learning sign language is a priority."

"Hey," says Zack.

"Whoa!" says Audrey. "Carson, what is your damage? Oh god, sorry, Nat! But Carson! Stop. I mean it, before I kick you in *the place*." There's a little hill of shredded napkin fluff in front of her.

"Guys," I say.

But Carson hasn't finished. "Let's put your, uh, *personal improvement* aside for a second, Leila, and think about what's really going on. Would you rather have your *sister* die or have her be a brain-damaged paraplegic? Isn't that more to the point?"

Everybody looks away from me. Silence.

"I don't have a sister," Leila finally says.

"Your weaselly little brother, then," snaps Audrey. "Though in some people's opinion he's brain-damaged already."

"Audrey!" says Zack.

"Oh god, sorry. Sorry, Nat. Reflex."

"I don't think . . ." I stop.

I don't know what I think or don't think. I'm hot and cold and numb all at once.

"It's not up to me," I whisper. "It's not like it's my choice."

New Entries

"Worst words," I say, to no one in particular. "*Statistic*. It's so prickly. And so is *optimistic*."

"Most pessimistic word ever," agrees Zack. "Only used when a disappointing outcome is expected."

"And *fluids*," I add.

"*Moist fluids,*" says Audrey.

"What other kind are there?" asks Carson.

"And *coma*," I say.

Family Meeting

Mom and Aunt Jeanie are at the table when I come in. Dad is shifting an aluminum-foiled pan in the oven.

"What's up?" I say.

Mom looks like the inside of her has been scraped out and she's drying up.

"Family meeting, Nat," says Dad. "Why don't you go wash your hands and we'll eat in five minutes."

Aunt Jeanie grabs and then pats me.

"My hands are clean," I say. "I was in the pool for four hours." I hold up my fingers. "Cleanest prunes in town."

Aunt Jeanie laughs way too hard. "You always were the funny one, Natalie."

Clunk. Silence. And which one was Claire? Pretty? Smart? Kind and loyal? And now? Which one is she now?

Mom moves my chair back so I'll sit down. Aunt Jeanie opens a bottle of red wine and puts a glass in front of me.

"No, Jeanie," says Mom, moving the glass. "She's sixteen."

"Don't you think she's old enough this week?" asks Jeanie. "If we lived in France . . ."

"I don't like it anyway," I say.

Dad pulls the pan out of the oven and almost drops it on the table. The pot holders are kind of shabby. Claire made them at camp, probably in the Elves cabin.

"You left the card on, Dad." I point to the charred rectangle taped to the casserole: *From the Bensons.*

Luckily, the Bensons are not here alongside their inedible broccoli-tofu slop, so we don't need to fake it past the first bite.

I clear the plates, except the wineglasses, which get refilled all round.

"So?" I say. "Family meeting?"

Mom looks at Dad; Dad looks at Mom; my aunt looks back and forth like she's watching tennis.

"Dr. Hazel spoke with your mother this afternoon," starts Dad. Aunt Jeanie grabs Mom's hand.

"Oh Christ," I say. "Just tell me."

"There's nothing to 'Just tell,' " says Dad.

"The results came back." Mom is talking slowly, making herself sound steady. "From the EEG. Dr. Hazel came to find me."

I go cold and I can't make my mouth work. I realize Dad and Jeanie already know. I realize this is all for me.

"Her brain . . . Claire's brain . . . it's dead, Natty. She died. Probably on Saturday night before we . . . when she . . ."

My eyes flood over watching Mom's do the same. I push back from the table, flinging my arms across my face.

No! Oh, Claire! Oh, Claire! *Claaaaaairrrrrre!*

It's me howling, but I don't know when it started. I feel hands all over me, trying to take hold, but I'm rocking, trying to speed through this part, shaking them off me, Don't make me be here anymore. . . .

I run to the bathroom and squat in front of the toilet. I flip up the seat. I put my palms on the sides of the cool bowl. I lean over, heaving, trying to puke. I heave deep in my gut, but my mouth is dry, dusty. There's a lump of something unbearable inside me but it won't come out.

What It Means

Not sure how long it takes, but later I'm ready to hear the rest.

My sister is dead.

Only she's still breathing.

Jeanie makes tea and dumps half the sugar bowl into my cup. "Brandy would be better," she says. Mom just looks at her and Jeanie turns red. Mom is older.

Claire was older.

There'll be no one to scold me with a *look* when I'm forty-three years old.

"Claire's heart . . ." Mom has to drag herself forward. "Claire's heart is healthy. It could continue to beat until . . . well, for fifty more years. Sixty, maybe, or more."

Claire's heart.

I get a flash of a valentine that Claire made when we were little. For me. Two paper hearts, sewn together around the edges with big lumpy wool stitches, and stuffed with those little cinnamon candies. *Luv* printed in big white letters.

"But it's only beating because the ventilator is providing oxygen. There are no natural functions working. If they . . . *when* they . . . remove the life-support system . . . she will . . . no longer be able to breathe."

"She'll be dead," I say, suddenly cold all over.

"She will die," says Dad.

"She's already dead," says Mom. "Really."

I look around for my hoodie. I'm shivering.

"So this . . . this is . . . *it*?" I say. "There's . . . no actual choice to make?"

Well, There Is One Thing

Mom and Dad look at each other. Aunt Jeanie opens her mouth, but Mom shakes her head.

"What?" I say. "What are you not telling me?"

"It's a difficult subject," says Mom.

"We're not sure you're ready for it," says Dad.

"Let's wait till a little later," says Aunt Jeanie. "But really, it has to be decided."

Wrapped in a Blanket, I Call Audrey from my Closet

"See, Claire was an adult, according to the law. Mom and Dad say what they think Claire would have wanted. And the hospital has to decide what her wishes would be."

"How the hell do they do that?"

"She checked that little box on her driver's license. She agreed to be an organ donor."

Anatomical Gifts

Claire and I never talked about it, not straight up. Why would we? We're *teenagers*.

They Might Be Okay

So we're in the car and Mom says, "George Casson called."

And Dad says, "George," in this fond, nostalgic way, and they look at each other, smiling, sharing some invisible thing.

"Who's George?" I say.

"We went to college with him," says Dad.

"We used to go camping," says Mom. And they *laugh*.

"Good old George," I say. But I have this disturbing flash that Mom and Dad are *friends*. They have memories that don't include Claire and me. How odd is that?

Is Someone Out There Waiting?

"The thing I keep wondering is . . ."

"What?" they all say.

"I keep wondering if someone out there is waiting for Claire to die."

"Ah," says Audrey.

"Of course," says Zack.

"Do you mind telling me what the hell you're talking about?" says Carson.

We're at Beanie's, iced coffee dregs melted into milky puddles at the bottoms of our glasses. I swirl mine, wanting to explain it the right way.

"Maybe there's some little boy who was born with a

hole in his heart," I say. "Or whatever. And they've kept him going all this time, but now he's ten, and if he doesn't get a heart transplant, he'll never see eleven. So with Claire's heart . . ."

"But wait! Then *she* won't see nineteen," says Carson.

"She won't see nineteen anyway," Zack says quietly.

"Claire's heart could save his life, this boy."

"Let's name him," says Audrey. "Let's call him . . . William."

"Not save just *his* life," I say. Maybe I'm trying to make it okay somehow, but, "Maybe William's supposed to grow up to do something really important. Maybe all the time he's spent in hospitals makes him grow up to be a brilliant doctor and he develops the cure for AIDS and all the billion children in Africa are saved."

"Yeah," says Audrey. "Thanks to Claire's heart."

"Good picture," says Zack.

"What else do they use?" says Carson. "Aside from the heart?"

"Carson!" says Leila.

"Kidneys," says Zack. "It's called harvesting. Big demand for healthy kidneys. All those people on dialysis. And the liver, the lungs, bone marrow . . . Pretty much everything can be used to help someone."

"Her skin," says Audrey. "They can graft her skin onto someone who's been burned."

"Oh!" I say. "What if someday I met someone who'd

been in a terrible fire and got all reconstructed, but I recognized some part of her arm, because Claire has these really distinctive freckles in a row on the top of her wrist, and they got stitched onto somebody else?"

"That's gruesome," says Leila.

"But so cool," says Audrey.

"That's gotta be the opening sequence for a horror movie," says Carson. "Where this deranged doctor—"

Audrey throws her spoon at him. "Shut up!"

"Shut *up*!" says Zack.

"What?" says Carson.

"You promised, you idiot." They glare at him.

"Oh." He glances at me and away. The tips of his ears go pink.

"Okay, okay," he says, after a minute. "But how about some loser kid who never made a goal in her life, maybe she could have Claire's right foot and turn into a soccer star?"

"Can they do a brain transplant?"

"Not yet, Leila," says Zack.

"You in the market for one?" says Carson. Then he stops. "Oh crap, I did it again."

I pat his hand. "It's okay, Carson. But what I'd like to know is what happens to Claire's *knowledge*? I keep wondering. Hours of studying! Where does her vocabulary go? Or her ability to kick the ball just the right way, to analyze the best defense in a split second? Or all those lyrics to every

Beatles song she memorized? Or, you know, just how to flip pancakes?"

"That what makes a person who she is," says Audrey. "That's what dies."

"That's what's unbearable."

I put my head on the table just as Zack says, "How about her eyes?"

Claire's Eyes

When I think about Claire's eyes, I see hazel pools with golden green flecks, framed by the best eyelashes a girl ever got. I see them crinkled up so tight while she laughs that she looks Asian. We even bought her a T-shirt one time: ASIAN GIRLS HAVE MORE FUN.

I know that whoever gets Claire's eyes, it won't actually be her eyes. They take the eyeballs from their sockets and harvest the corneas for use by some old blind person.

"Oh!" Carson would say. "That would be an awesome movie! What if a person got someone else's eyes, and suddenly had all the memories of everything the eyes had ever seen?"

But in real life it won't be like seeing the world through Claire's eyes. Just a second chance.

thursday

Today

I wake up. I wake up remembering that old rhyme about birthdays: Wednesday's child is full of woe. Thursday's child has far to go. It's about *birth*days, but I'm thinking how far Claire is going to go today.

Full of *woe*. I don't even want to open my eyes. I press my face into Claire's pillow, using it to soak up the tears that feel like steam behind my lids.

Any Chance She Knows?

We must believe utterly that there is no brain activity at all. Period. That Claire is dead. And we're just . . . releasing her body from the confines of medicine.

But the body is one thing, right? What about her spirit? Is there such a thing? Is there a Claire angel hovering over her body, watching this going on? When I was talking to her all week, I was talking to the body, just in case it would keep her on earth somehow to hear my voice. But what if . . . There I go again, *what if* she's listening in some other way?

And when we turn off the machine . . . where will she go?

Last Night We Talked About Heaven

"Of course there's a heaven," says Leila. "If heaven doesn't exist, how can it have a name? And all those pictures of it?"

"Uh, Leila?" says Audrey. "That would be Im. Ag. In. Ary. . . . How can people in heaven tell us what heaven looks like? They're *dead*."

"Well, how come so many artists have the same ideas?" Leila asks, like she's scoring some winning point. "The paintings all show choirs of angels wearing floaty robes. God has a white beard like Dumbledore, and it's blue up there, with creamy clouds and no red except Christ's lips. Someone must have seen it!"

"First of all, Leila, there is no god," says Audrey. "And, secondly, *if* there is one, he's not . . . wait, *she's* not . . . no, actually, if there is one, he's clearly male because he's messing up so bad. . . . So anyway, he's not sitting on a lawn chair in the sky, surveying his kingdom from the deck of a cruise ship, deciding who gets into heaven."

"How do you know?"

"Sounds dull as doggy-do," says Carson. "Hell at least has sinners."

"Hell is a state of mind," says Zack, quoting his favorite T-shirt.

"Hell is taking chemistry over and over, never passing the exam," says Leila.

"I think hell would be something so simple," says Audrey. "Like . . ." She pokes Carson's shoulder. "Like . . ." She keeps poking him, every two seconds. "Getting poked for eternity. Wouldn't that just drive you *insane*?" Poke.

"Quit it," says Carson. Poke. "I mean it." Poke. He swats her.

"So then it follows that heaven is different for everyone too," says Zack.

"Well, mine would have lap dancers and fireworks," says Carson.

"Mine would be a bookstore," says Zack. "With towering stacks and dust and rare books no one has opened in a hundred years."

Carson is staring at him. "You really are a loser," he says. "How are you ever going to get laid?"

"I wish there could be angels," says Audrey, rescuing

her brother. "But my heaven is an ecolodge in Costa Rica, with a jungle and awesome mynah birds and waterfalls. And the angels would be like tour guides who could show you the mother howler monkey or warn you about the coral snake draped in the emerald canopy."

"There wouldn't be any coral snakes," I say. "If it's heaven. No pain, no sorrow, no venom and no serpents."

"Oh. Yeah. But coral snakes are so incredible to look at, so maybe they've just been . . . devenomized."

"What's your heaven, Nat?" Zack asks.

What would I want for eternity?

"Mine would be . . . that there could be miracles once in a while here on earth. That you didn't have to wait till later."

What Do You Wear?

Mom says no shorts. It's a hundred freaking degrees outside. I put on Claire's gray linen pants and her black thingy.

Mom is wearing a silk blouse, pale blue. "Claire gave me this," she says, smoothing it down over her skirt.

"I did too."

She hugs me. "Of course you did."

Dad's in a suit. I tell him, "Dad. You might want to be relaxed, take off the tie."

"Relaxed?" he says.

We Pull Out of the Driveway

Audrey and Zack are standing at attention at the corner, their bikes propped against the lamppost. They're both wearing black and they're each holding a red balloon. Audrey has tears streaming down her face and they blow kisses and wave.

"You sure have nutty friends," says Dad, and he toots the horn to say thanks.

Aunt Jeanie Goes In

I watch through the window. She stands there with her fingers resting on Claire's shoulder. She doesn't speak but just looks, for a pretty long time. Then she leans over and kisses Claire's forehead. She comes out, wiping her eyes.

I feel like there's an order, that I'm next, that Dad and Mom have to come after me; they've known her longer than I have. I go in.

My Turn

I don't know how to tell you goodbye. You're my closest person in the world . . . and how can this be the end?

I love you, Claire, so much that I didn't even notice until this happened. All the words are clichéd but that's all I have, aside from this huge ache in my chest.

You're as much a part of me as my own skin.

I will miss you forever.

I will never stop thinking of things to tell you.

I will never stop wishing you were with me.

I will never stop loving you, ever.

I know now that you can't hear me. But I wish that . . . somehow . . . you could . . . *absorb* . . . my, my *reverberations* . . . take some of me with you, like you're leaving . . . your *self* with me. So I'm . . . sending *me* . . . with you. . . .

I guess that's all.

G'bye.

Mwa.

And I Leave

Dad hugs me when I get outside and then he goes in. Mom hugs me and follows Dad. Jeanie is waiting in the lounge. I see the chaplain guy lurking by the nurses' station, with his dark jacket and his solemn eyebrows, but that doesn't stop me. I slide down the wall next to a laundry trolley and I sob like a baby, with my butt on the hard, cool floor and my face hiding in a stack of clean sheets. There's an orderly next to a gurney right there and I realize he's waiting to take . . . the *body* away, right after. To get cut up, and distributed into coolers and hurried to . . . William, and the other patients waiting for their lives to be saved.

I go into the bathroom to splash my face and try to calm down for Phase Two, but the water doesn't get icy enough and I'm basically soaking my shirt. Claire's shirt. So I go back and they're waiting for me. Dad has signaled the nurses that we're ready.

The Send-off

Trisha is setting up chairs next to Claire's bed. The monitor thing has been moved away to make space. Mom sits on the right and Dad sits on the left, close to her head. I climb onto the bed. Mom and Dad look worried at each other but Trisha just nods it's okay.

This Claire's body is not the familiar one I've spooned a million times. And she's on her back, not curled to make a sister nest. But I'd rather be here than anywhere. I do the best I can to lie beside her and stay on the bed. Lucky I'm skinny. I put my head oh so gently on her rib cage and close my eyes.

They said it won't take long, they said just a few minutes. As soon as the ventilator stops sending in oxygen, the rest of the system shuts down.

I keep my eyes shut and try not to listen to anything except the beating of her heart. The doctor comes in and there's some murmuring and I know they've turned off the machine because the *beep* stops.

They said it's not like a death from natural causes,

where the patient is struggling to breathe, where the time between inhalations gets longer and the breaths themselves can sound like faulty motors. They said it would be easy.

There's rustling around me, and sniffling, but mostly there's just this distant drum inside Claire.

But then it's fainter and then hardly there. And then it's not there at all. I guess I'm the first one to know, because I'm listening to nothing.

Another minute goes by. There's movement around me. Someone lifts Claire's hand. I'm more aware of being uncomfortable, but I don't want to get up yet. I sure don't want to open my eyes.

And then the doctor's voice. "The patient has died. Time of death is 12:16 p.m."

Definition

It'll all be *later* now, won't it? It'll be either "when Claire was alive" or "after Claire died."

After Claire Died

Being a grown-up means somehow knowing how to arrange a funeral. That's what Mom and Jeanie do. Dad answers the phone the four hundred times it rings. Everyone's been waiting to hear, and we're the ones who know.

I hear him say it over and over: "She died peacefully at

noon today. We were all with her. Natalie is doing fine, thanks. We're all doing fine. It was for the best."

For the best, eh? For the better-than-worst, anyway.

Uncle Denny comes and Dad's brother, Mike, comes again, this time with his boyfriend, Arlen. Claire and I like Arlen, almost more than Mike. Grandpa John will get here for the funeral. Other family too, they'll all come. This is the family tragedy of the century. Gina and Maeve and Shelley and all the neighbors trickle in. There's so much food that Jeanie takes some over to the food bank.

It's all after Claire died, but it's *right* after Claire died, so I don't know what it's like yet. I lie on my bed.

tuesday

The Funeral

They all come to the funeral. Zack and Carson even wear suits. Leila's in black, but she's featuring a cleavage you wouldn't expect at a moment of bereavement. Audrey decides to go with a white flowing gown, as a salute to the angels that she wishes could be greeting Claire at the other end.

I look around and see probably every person Claire has ever had a conversation with. There aren't enough seats. There are a million flowers, and it's hot, like a party in a Southern novel, with the women fanning themselves and the sweet smell of freesias floating over the assortment of black-clothed armpit blasts.

Joe-boy comes with his dad; Kate comes with her mother; Taylor comes with her evil mother, Mrs. Flint. The chapel place is full of crying women and we sing Claire off to heaven. Or wherever.

Back at the House

I don't really remember when my grandmother died, except that I wore a navy blue dress with red piping, which, at the age of eight, I was afraid might be blasphemous. I remember being with Claire afterward, passing plates of sandwiches to a hundred old ladies with draping flesh, hearing over and over how sweet we were.

The sandwiches are here, but Claire isn't. There are a few old ladies dotted around, but mostly a hundred kids from school, and everyone else too. And relatives, of course. The house is packed.

My skin has been prickling since I got dressed, as if I wrapped myself in sandpaper. It's hot, really hot, and the AC isn't doing its thing because of so many people coming in and out.

If it weren't his daughter's wake, Dad'd be yelling to Closethedamndoor.Don'tyoukidsknowhowmuchitcoststo coolanoldhouseforyourgoddamncomfort?

I look over and see Gina laughing at something Audrey said. Laughing so much she actually throws her head back and shows her long throat and her teeth. Wow, I think. She had a dead baby and now she's laughing.

Audrey can be pretty funny, I guess.

Another Thing That Would Not Have Happened a Week Ago

Zack comes up and puts his arm around my shoulder.
"Is it in bad taste to say you look cute in mourning?"
He gets a hip check, but I'm smiling too.

Night

We can only squish four into the hammock on the front porch, so it's a good thing Leila went home with her parents. If any of us moves we'll notice whose knee is jabbing whose spine and whose elbow is under whose neck. So we don't move at all; only the hammock, rocking, rocking, lulls us into feeling that today has come to a peaceful end.

many weeks later
september 19

What Didn't Happen

"I was awake all night," says Mom. She's waving a spatula.

"I can see that." There are dozens and dozens of chocolate chip cookies laid out on newspaper sheets, on the table, on the counter, on top of the microwave.

"It's Claire's birthday," says Mom.

"I know."

"She was supposed to be away at college and I would have packed a huge box of cookies . . . and I would have stuck in some balloons and some party hats . . . and those little paper blow things that squeak. . . ."

I put my arm around Mom's shoulder because she's starting to shake.

"And I would have been so sad, 'cause she wasn't home for her birthday for the first time in her life. . . ."

We stand there, holding on for a minute.

"But it didn't . . . ," she mumbles, wiping her eyes.

"No . . ."

We give it a little more time. We've had some practice by now, in these kinds of moments.

"So, Mom," I finally say. "About the baking."

She laughs. "Maybe you can bring your friends over after school? For milk and cookies?"

Wish I Could Text Claire

happy bday old face

We Find a Way to Observe

They all know what day it is, which is why we're in the park on a school night.

I've been struggling with myself since leaving my mother in the kitchen this morning, trying not to think about Claire. But that seems like the wrong idea, not to mention ridiculous and impossible.

So, I'm letting *sad* soak into me, getting drenched in Claire's not being here.

"Tell your mother I want to marry her," says Carson. He's eaten half the cookies.

Audrey kicks him. "It feels like we should be doing something special," she says.

"Let's do the pools," says Zack. "That's the last time we hung out with Claire before she . . . before the accident."

"Yes!" I say. That's exactly what I want to do.

None of us has a swimsuit but we don't care.

"Is the singer girl away?"

"Pretty sure."

"Let's just go there. Then we can loiter."

I haven't been swimming since I stopped work for school. Now I can't wait.

I zoom ahead of the others on my bike. I can hear them trying to catch up. I park the bike and dash down the driveway, through the gate into the shadows of the backyard.

The owner is away, so the pool is unlit. I take off my shorts and top and slide into the dark, secret water.

I'm only by myself for a minute, time to look up at the watery moon from the underside of the surface.

And then they all come jumping in: Audrey first, of course, and then the others, turning the pool into a party for Claire's birthday.

Maybe *Party* Is the Wrong Word

I ride home alone. The night's still warm, and always quiet in a small town. There is no reason to believe that I'll hurt less someday. Someday it'll be me Mom is sending cookies to, me Mom and Dad are missing, me starting a new life full of people who never met Claire. Will that be better or worse?

Pretending for a Minute That I'm a Poet

I've decided that hope is an ever-changing element, like water.

It calls to you; it beckons; you want to plunge right in. But it's treacherous too; it tricks you and swallows you up.

If you told me this whole story and it didn't happen to me? I'd say *screw* hope—if you stick a hopeful ending on there, it'll be a total lie.

But what I know about water is that after all the splashing and the churning, it lies still. It quenches your thirst and it buoys you up.

So I guess I'll be one of those wobbly-pegged, flappy-skinned old ladies at the Y, because I'm going to be swimming until I really can't anymore.

I'll be the Driftwood of the future, paddling along on my own.

A Happy Ending?

Nowhere near happy.

And, except for Claire, not really an ending at all.

Acknowledgments

Huge thanks to friends who provided important details for this story:

Dr. Ruben Olmedo, Ingrid Stenskar, Carly Huitema, Marianne Huitema, Hannah Jocelyn, and Nell Jocelyn